Books in the Replica series

Look out for:

Book 6

And the Two Shall Meet

Marilyn Kaye

Hodder
Children's
Books

a division of Hodder Headline

First published as a Bantam Skylark paperback in the
USA in 1998 by Bantam, Doubleday Dell
Publishing Group Inc, USA

This paperback edition published in Great Britain in 2000
by Hodder Children's Books

10 9 8 7 6 5 4 3 2 1

A Catalogue record for this book
is available from the British Library

ISBN 0340 74956 3

Typeset by Hewer Text Ltd, Edinburgh
Printed and bound in Great Britain by
Clays Ltd, St Ives plc

Hodder Children's Books
A Division of Hodder Headline
338 Euston Road
London NW1 3BH

For the cousins of November 1998:
Alice Clerc, Augustin Clerc, Zoë Huybrechts

1

The remains of Sunday breakfast were still on the kitchen table, but Eric ignored the plates he was supposed to be clearing with his sister, Tasha. Instead, he examined the brochure that was spread out on the table. By now he practically knew every word by heart, but he never got tired of looking at the colour pictures.

One photo in particular entranced him. It was of a canoe careening over a raging river. Inside, three teenagers, two boys and a girl, gripped their paddles as they sailed over the white foam. The picture captured the thrill of the moment, and Eric felt a shiver of happy anticipation.

His sister peered over his shoulder at the picture. 'What are they doing?' she asked.

'White-water rafting,' he told her. 'Man, I can't wait to do that.'

'Why?'

'Because it's exciting! It's a rush!'

'It doesn't look exciting to me,' Tasha commented. 'That canoe looks like it's about to tip over. Two seconds after this photo was taken, those three kids probably fell out and drowned.'

Eric snorted. 'They didn't drown, Tasha. There's never been a fatality in a Wilderness Adventure outing.'

'Not yet,' Tasha said darkly. 'There's always a first time. Hey, if you drown, can I have your stereo?'

Eric ignored that comment and pointed to another picture. 'See that girl? She can't be any older than you are, and look what she's doing.'

'She's climbing a mountain,' Tasha said. 'So what?'

'So wouldn't you like to scale great heights?'

'No,' Tasha said, and left the room.

Eric sighed. Personally, he didn't really care whether or not his sister came along on the Wilderness Adventure outing. But Amy had her heart set on Tasha joining them, so he was doing his best to talk her into it. Unfortunately, Tasha wasn't exactly the outdoorsy type.

He'd first heard about Wilderness Adventure way

back in September, from a couple of friends at school who'd just returned from a summer hiking and rock climbing expedition. From that moment on, he was determined to have one of the world-famous experiences. Wilderness Adventure offered teen programmes in the mountains, on rivers, in the desert, all over the United States and Canada, and featured adventures ranging from mountain climbing to deep-sea diving, from skiing to boating. There were weekend programmes, month-long programmes, and everything in between.

Eric hadn't immediately started nagging his parents to send him. He had planned his approach carefully. First, he gathered all the information he could find on Wilderness Adventure, all its credentials and recommendations from other nationally known youth organisations. He'd even managed to find a documentary video about the experience. Armed with all this, plus the phone numbers of the parents who'd sent their kids, he'd presented the plan to his parents.

He'd pointed out the goals of Wilderness Adventure, how it stressed self-esteem, confidence building, survival skills, and responsible behaviour. His parents were impressed. He didn't mention that his own personal goal was to have a good time.

A rap on the kitchen window make him look up. He rose and opened the back door. It was Amy.

'What are you up to?' she asked as she came in.

'Looking at the brochure,' he admitted, feeling a little silly.

'Again?' But her grin told him she understood completely. She pulled a chair over to sit beside him at the table and pored over the pictures. 'Can you believe it? In one week, this will be us.'

'What *I* can't believe,' Eric replied, 'is your mother actually letting you go.'

'She's still not exactly thrilled about it,' Amy said. Amy's mother was a little overprotective, more so than an ordinary mother, and Eric understood why. Amy wasn't an ordinary daughter.

'You know, you're probably safer out in the wilderness than you are right here in Los Angeles,' he remarked. 'We'll be in the middle of nowhere. Those creeps won't be able to watch you.'

'That's true,' Amy conceded. 'But my mom is still nervous about the same stuff any parent would be nervous about. Rock climbing, rafting . . . those activities can be dangerous.'

'For *you*?' Eric asked in disbelief. 'Not possible.'

Amy grinned. 'Sure. I'm not invulnerable, you know.'

'Just a little less vulnerable than the rest of us,' Eric teased. 'Hey, what happens to a clone when she falls off a mountain?'

'She breaks bones like everyone else,' Amy said. 'I'm still a human being, you know. Just . . . just . . .' She fumbled, as if searching for the right word to describe herself.

Eric helped out. 'Stronger,' he said. 'And smarter, and faster. Not to mention the fact that you can see and hear better than any ordinary human being.'

Amy couldn't deny any of that, but she whispered, 'Keep your voice down.'

'My parents are out,' Eric assured her. 'It's just me and Tasha here. Don't worry, I'm not about to give away your little secret.'

Amy raised her eyebrows. 'My *little* secret?'

Eric knew what she was implying. When a person wasn't born the normal way, but cloned from superior genetic material in a laboratory – well, 'a little secret' was an understatement. It was a *big* secret, and not because Amy was ashamed of or embarrassed by her unusual makeup.

Eric could still remember his own reaction when

5

Amy first told him her history. Here was this cute next-door neighbour, his sister's best friend, whom he'd known practically all his life, telling him she was in danger of being captured by people intent on using her to create a master race.

She wasn't even sure who these people were. All she knew was that they were part of an organisation that had originally funded the government cloning experiment just over twelve years earlier. The scientists involved with the actual project thought they were doing research to find the causes and cures for genetic disorders. Upon learning the real motives of the organisation, the scientists destroyed the laboratory and all the evidence of what they'd been doing – except for the tiny clones. Those infants had been sent all over the world, hopefully to be adopted and raised as normal people who would never know they were different. No one anticipated that around the age of puberty, the twelve Amy clones would begin to realise how different they were.

Amy had been taken by one of the scientists – Nancy Candler, the woman she considered her mother. Like the other scientists, Nancy had assumed that the organisation would believe the clones had perished in the laboratory explosion.

But incidents in recent months had made it clear that their attempt at deception hadn't worked. Amy could never be completely safe.

So Eric was a little surprised that Ms Candler was allowing Amy to go off on this summer adventure. 'I'll bet she checked Wilderness Adventure out pretty carefully,' he remarked.

'No kidding,' Amy affirmed. 'I'm lucky it's such a well-known programme. Even so, she made a zillion phone calls before she was sure it was for real. And now, she doesn't stop lecturing me to be careful.'

'As if she has anything to worry about,' Eric said. 'You know you'll be the most talented athlete in the group.' He didn't bother to conceal the pride in his voice.

'That's the problem,' Amy reminded him. 'You know what my mother's always telling me. "Don't be too good," "Don't stand out." I'm not supposed to call attention to myself.'

Eric had heard all this before. 'Well, unless we have a superhero in the group, you'll still be the best,' he said confidently.

'Probably,' she acknowledged. 'But I have to make sure I don't show off and let the others know I can do stuff normal people can't do.'

'But what if you *have* to show off?' Eric asked her.

'What do you mean?'

'Well, let's say we've just climbed a mountain, and we're standing on the edge of a cliff. I trip and start to go over the edge. Just as I'm about to tumble to a horrible death, you grab my ankle and pull me back up the cliff. Now, a normal twelve-year-old girl wouldn't have that much strength, right? So everyone will know there's something different about you.'

Amy nodded slowly. 'That's true.'

'You wouldn't let me fall just to protect your secret, would you?' he asked with mock anxiety.

Amy looked thoughtful, as if considering the problem. 'I've got the solution,' she said suddenly. She grinned. 'Don't trip.'

'Thanks a lot.' Eric laughed. 'Hey, I've got a question for you. When someone's been cloned from genetically superior material, are they super-resistant to tickling?' Not waiting for an answer, he grabbed her waist.

'Stop it!' Shrieking and giggling at the same time, Amy pushed him away and then fell into his lap.

'What's so funny?' Tasha asked, ambling into the kitchen.

'Eric is mad because he thinks I won't save him

when he falls off a mountain,' Amy told her. 'What do you think I should do?'

Tasha didn't even bother to consider the question. 'Let him drop,' she replied promptly.

Eric made a face at his sister. Amy playfully ruffled his hair: 'Don't worry, Eric, I'll take care of you. Even if it means letting all of Wilderness Adventure know that they have a clone in their midst.'

'How many people will be in your group?' Tasha asked them.

'We don't know for sure,' Amy said. 'According to the brochure, the groups are always small, never more than eight. Plus counsellors. There's one counsellor for every three participants. The counsellors are supposed to be excellent. They take all these gruelling tests for special certification before Wilderness Adventure sends them out on treks.'

'What if someone really does fall off a mountain?' Tasha wondered.

'That can't happen,' Amy said firmly. 'It's completely safe; you've got ropes and stuff. You couldn't fall off if you jumped.'

'Okay, but they can't stop someone from just tripping and hitting their head on a rock,' Tasha pointed out.

'All the counsellors have the same training as paramedics in the fire department,' Amy declared. 'It says so right in the brochure. Anyway, Tasha, you can trip and hit your head on your own front steps! You're probably safer at Wilderness Adventure, where the counsellors can fix you up.'

'At least I can't fall out of a raft and drown on my own front steps,' Tasha countered.

Amy groaned. 'Honestly, Tasha, do you think thousands of parents would let their kids go off on these programmes if it wasn't safe?'

Eric knew what Amy was doing. She was still trying to convince Tasha to come along with them. Tasha had realised this too, but she ignored Amy and opened the fridge. 'Anyone want something to eat?' she asked.

'We just had breakfast,' Eric pointed out.

'Yeah, I know,' Tasha said. She closed the refrigerator door.

'Tasha,' Amy wheedled. 'Doesn't this sound cool?' She picked up the brochure and read aloud. ' "Be your very best! Challenge yourself! Realise your potential! Achieve, succeed, and discover yourself!" '

'Actually, I wouldn't mind a little orange juice,' Tasha said, reopening the refrigerator.

Amy went on. ' "Develop skills you never knew

you had. Take risks you never thought you'd take." Tasha, are you listening to me?'

This time, Tasha slammed the refrigerator door with a bang. 'Have you been listening to *me*?' she shouted. 'This isn't my kind of thing! I'm not an athlete!'

'But you don't have to be an athlete,' Amy persisted. 'Listen.' She began reading again. ' "Wilderness Adventure outings are designed for young people who are generally healthy, with average physical capabilities. No special skills are required for participation." See, you just have to be normal!'

'Normal?' Eric repeated. 'Forget it, Tasha. Ow!'

Amy had given his shoulder a sharp pinch, and it seemed that she had forgotten to control her strength. Or maybe not. In any case, Eric resolved to stay out of the discussion.

But Amy hadn't given up. She stood, pulled Tasha into the adjoining dining room, and shut the sliding door. Eric couldn't hear their discussion.

It was just as well. Even though he kept telling himself he didn't care whether or not Tasha came along, he was actually a little peeved at his sister for being such a wimp about it all. It was weird – Tasha could be so brave and aggressive about some things, like writing controversial articles for the school newspaper and arguing her point of view and confronting people who offended her. He remembered when they were in New York, and Amy was poisoned . . . Tasha was ready to storm the hospital when she thought Amy was in trouble. But it was true, Tasha wasn't a jock. She didn't like phys ed, and she'd recently dropped out of gymnastics when the routines became too advanced for her.

So he guessed he understood why she was wimping out. She was probably more afraid of looking foolish in front of others than of being in any actual danger. Amy was wasting her time.

Which was why he was completely surprised when the girls emerged from the dining room and Amy announced, 'Tasha's going with us.'

'You're kidding!' Eric exclaimed.

Tasha wouldn't look at him directly as she spoke. 'Amy says she'll help me with anything I can't do, even if it means revealing her powers.'

'Oh yeah?' He looked at Amy. 'You mean you'd give up your secret for her but not for me?'

Amy put an arm around Tasha. 'Hey, she was my best friend long before you became my boyfriend.'

Eric turned to Tasha. 'So that's it? Just because she says she'll help you, you changed your mind?'

'Well, there was more,' Tasha acknowledged. 'Amy said if I don't go, she won't go.'

'What?' Eric yelped in disbelief.

'So you owe me a great big thank you for changing my mind,' Tasha told him. 'I have to go see if my old hiking boots still fit.' She left them in the kitchen and ran upstairs.

Eric stared at Amy. 'You didn't mean what you told her, did you?' he demanded. 'You wouldn't have deserted me like that!'

Amy smiled sweetly. 'What does that matter now? She's coming with us, and everything's fine.'

Eric rolled his eyes. 'Yeah, okay.' But then another thought occurred to him. 'Wait a minute. There might not be room for her in our group. I'll bet they've filled up by now.'

'There's room for Tasha,' Amy replied smugly. 'She was registered when we were. I told your parents I'd talk her into going.'

'How could you be so sure of that?'

Amy grinned. 'I'm a super-convincer, that's why.'

Once again, Eric shook his head in awe and admiration and thought about how lucky he was. How many other guys had girlfriends who never stopped amazing them?

2

A my peered out the window of the Winnebago as it flew down the two-lane highway.
The traffic was sparse now, and any sign of a city
had disappeared long ago. From the passenger side
in the front seat, a young woman with wire-
rimmed glasses and a halo of blonde curls turned
to look at the group riding in the back.

'How's everyone doing?' she asked with a wide,
warm smile.

'Fine,' the six people chorused automatically.

'No one's feeling carsick?'

The chorus replied, 'No.'

'You're lucky,' the young woman said. 'For me,
this is the worst part of every expedition. I can walk
across a swinging rope bridge a hundred feet above

jagged rocks, but long car rides make me positively dizzy. And you've all been doing a lot of travelling today, haven't you?'

Amy could certainly nod at that, for her and Tasha and Eric. They'd left the apartment block where they all lived at eight o'clock that morning. Amy's mother took them to the airport, where they boarded a flight to San Francisco. There, they were met by their Wilderness Adventure counsellors, Flora and Dallas, along with three other participants. They'd taken off in a van and had now been on the road for seven hours. They were just crossing the state line into Oregon.

'When do we get there?' a pretty girl sitting across from Amy asked.

'We'll be out of this van in less than two hours,' Flora told them. 'Then it's a six-mile hike to the base camp.'

Amy could see Tasha struggling to keep back a groan of dismay. Apparently Flora could see that too. She flashed her warm smile again. 'Don't worry, it's not a rigorous hike.'

'That's right.' This confirmation came from Dallas, who was driving the van. 'As long as you don't mind climbing at a ninety-degree angle.'

Flora laughed and gave Dallas a light punch on the arm. 'Now, stop that,' she scolded him playfully. She turned back to the group. 'Don't listen to him, it's his first time on this particular expedition. Actually, it's a very easy walk to the camp, practically flat all the way. We don't want to wipe you out the first day!'

'What about the second?' That question came from a tall, gangly boy whose complexion was unusually pale for someone from California.

'Well, you're here to challenge yourself, right?' Flora asked him.

The boy said nothing, but there was no mistaking the trepidation in his eyes.

'Let's use this time to get to know each other,' Flora suggested. 'First of all, let me make sure I have everyone's names right.' She nodded towards the pretty girl. 'You're Brooke, right?'

'Yes.'

She went on to identify the others. 'Andy, Willard, Amy, Eric, and Tanya, right?'

'It's Tasha,' Tasha corrected her, 'not Tanya.'

'Sorry about that,' Flora said. 'But I can guarantee you, I won't call you by the wrong name again. It's one of the rules of Wilderness Adventure. It's okay to make a mistake, but we never make the same mistake twice.'

'How long have you been a counsellor?' Amy asked.

'Six years,' Flora told her, and she was clearly proud as she added, 'and fifty expeditions! Including four on this particular programme.'

'This is your first expedition, Dallas?' Eric asked.

'Oh, no,' Dallas said quickly. 'I'm not a complete amateur! But I've only been a full-fledged counsellor for six months, and this is my first trip on this route. That's why I've been teamed with a more experienced member of the organisation.'

Amy had a feeling that wasn't the only reason they'd been teamed together – not if Dallas and Flora had had anything to do with the decision. She hadn't missed the looks they occasionally exchanged. It was the same way she and Eric sometimes glanced at each other when no one was watching. In her opinion, there was definitely something more than Wilderness Adventure between them. Which was good; maybe they'd be understanding if she and Eric occasionally wandered away from the others.

So far, everyone seemed okay. Brooke, with her

bright eyes and her sun-bleached hair pulled back in a ponytail, looked like the sporty type. Amy hadn't been too crazy about the way her eyes had lingered on Eric when they first met, but Amy thought she was probably the boy-crazy type. In fact, Brooke had looked at Andy in the same way when they were introduced.

The same didn't apply to Willard, though. But Willard wasn't much to look at. Tall and scrawny, Willard had the appearance of a boy who'd grown very suddenly and wasn't sure what to do with his arms and legs any more. He had some acne on his chin too. Amy didn't hold that against him – even Eric sometimes got an eruption or two. Amy was hoping that her special genes would protect her from pimples in the years to come.

Andy was zit-free. He was a good-looking guy, with heavy-lidded dark blue eyes and blond hair naturally streaked with gold from the sun. He hadn't said much since they'd all been together in the van, but they'd all been pretty quiet. Amy thought it was a combination of nervous excitement, fear of the unknown, and the normal shyness people feel when confronted with strangers.

'Let's find out more about each other,' Flora suggested. 'Willard, where are you from?'

Willard named a town Amy had never heard of, but Flora seemed familiar with it and nodded in approval. 'There's some great skiing up there!'

'I guess,' Willard said. 'I don't ski.'

'What do you like to do?'

'Video games,' he said. 'Computer games. And I collect comics.'

'What kind?' Eric asked.

'Superman, Batman, and Spider-Man.'

'So you're interested in superheroes,' Flora commented.

'Yeah.'

Brooke turned to him. 'Is that why you decided to join up with Wilderness Adventure? So you could act out some superhero fantasies?' Her tone was perfectly innocent, but Amy got the feeling she was mocking Willard. He had the kind of pallor that meant he didn't spend a lot of time outdoors, and she guessed that maybe he really didn't want to be here at all, that his parents were making him do this. In any case, he didn't answer Brooke's question, just shrugged, and made it clear he didn't really want to talk.

Flora got the message. 'What about you, Brooke? Tell us something about yourself.'

Brooke clearly didn't mind talking. In the next few minutes, they learned that she was an eighth-grader from a town near San Francisco, with interests that ranged from diving to gymnastics. 'I've just started spelunking,' she added.

'What's spelunking?' Amy asked.

'Exploring caves,' Brooke told her.

'That sounds scary,' Tasha blurted out.

'I love to take risks,' Brooke said. 'I'm into danger.'

Amy could practically feel Tasha's shudder. She thought Flora would be pleased to hear what Brooke was telling them, but the counsellor actually frowned slightly.

'Taking risks can be good,' she said, 'but they should be realistic risks. And no one should be looking for danger. Keep in mind, people, there's a big difference between bravery and foolishness. What do you think of that, Eric?'

'I'll try not to be too foolish,' Eric said, and grinned. 'But I don't know how brave I'll be either!'

Dallas, with his eyes on the road, called out a

comment. 'No one knows that until the moment comes when your bravery is tested.'

Flora nodded in agreement. 'What else can you tell us about yourself, Eric?'

'Well, I like running,' he said. 'I'm on the track team at school, and I'm a forward on the basketball team.'

Brooke looked at him with bright eyes. 'High school?'

'No, middle school.'

'Oh.' She looked away. Eric flushed slightly, but Amy was pleased to see that Brooke had lost interest in him.

Flora, however, was nodding with approval. 'Team-work will be very important in our adventure,' she told Eric. 'Andy, what about you?'

'I'm at high school in San Francisco,' he told the group. 'I play a fair amount of tennis.'

'I *knew* it!' Brooke declared triumphantly. 'I could tell you were a tennis player.'

'How?' Tasha asked her.

'His arms! You've got great definition, Andy.'

Amy thought that Brooke was just trying to embarrass the guy, but it was true that Andy was a little more muscular than the average teenage boy.

He just smiled. 'Well, I'm not a pro or anything. My dad's got some weights in the basement that I fool around with sometimes.'

'I used to live in San Francisco,' Brooke continued. 'What high school do you go to?'

'The Clayton Academy.'

'Oh!' Brooke's eyes widened but she said no more.

Tasha went next. 'I'm in the seventh grade at Parkside Middle School in Los Angeles. I write for the school newspaper, and . . . and . . . I don't know what else to say about myself.'

'And she's my best friend,' Amy piped up. 'And Eric's sister. And a very cool person.'

Tasha smiled at her gratefully. 'I guess I should tell everyone right now, I'm kind of a klutz. I took gymnastics for a long time, but I hate sports. So I'm a little nervous about this.'

Flora spoke reassuringly. 'It's natural to be nervous,' she told Tasha. 'And this *will* be a challenge for you, but you'll emerge from this experience feeling more empowered than you ever thought you could feel. Amy?'

'I'm a seventh-grader at Parkside Middle School in Los Angeles too,' Amy declared. 'Just like Tasha.'

Flora smiled. 'And would you call yourself a klutz too?'

Amy avoided Eric's eyes and tried to think of what to say. Flora misunderstood the silence. 'This is a great opportunity to extend yourself,' she said. 'But I promise you, no one will be forced to do anything they can't do. Remember, the first goal of Wilderness Adventure is to have fun.'

Dallas left the highway then and pulled the van into the tiny parking area of a small convenience store.

'Everyone out!' he called. 'There are rest rooms behind the store, and we'll be stocking up on some water for the hike.'

Amy, Tasha, and Brooke found themselves side by side, washing their hands in the rest room. Amy tried to think of something casual to say that would lead to easy conversation between them.

'It's a small group,' she noted. 'Smaller than I thought it would be.'

Brooke nodded, 'Two friends of mine from school were supposed to be coming, but they both got the flu and had to drop out at the last minute.'

Amy didn't want her to think she and Tasha would be too exclusive. 'Well, it'll still be fun for you.'

'Oh, sure,' Brooke said. 'It looks like a good group. That Willard's a dork, but Eric seems okay.'

'More than okay,' Amy murmured.

'And Andy's cool,' Brooke continued. 'I can't believe he goes to the Clayton Academy.'

'Why?' Tasha asked. 'Is it special?'

Brooke nodded. 'It's for super-intelligent types. You have to pass these massive tests to get in. I always thought the kids who went there would be intellectual nerds. Andy doesn't look like the type.'

Thinking of poor Willard, Amy said, 'Well, I guess it's not a good idea to make snap judgments based on the way people look.'

'I'm an excellent judge of character,' Brooke informed her. 'Everyone says so. I can figure people out very quickly. That's why no one can ever keep any secrets from me.' With that, she dried her hands and sauntered out of the rest room.

Tasha looked at Amy worriedly. 'I hope she doesn't start trying to figure *you* out.'

Amy wasn't concerned. 'I think she'll be much more interested in figuring out Andy.'

When they returned to the parking area, they found that their backpacks had been taken out of the van. Since they had each received precise instructions on what to buy and bring, the packs were identical: green nylon around an aluminum frame. Amy assumed that the others had the same stuff packed inside their packs – clothes, food, and cooking gear in the big compartment; personal small stuff like soap and toothbrushes in the smaller pockets. Rolled tightly and strapped to the outside of the frame were the sleeping bags. Sitting on the ground, the packs looked huge and unwieldy, but once hers was on her back, Amy found that it wasn't bad at all – not too heavy, and the curves in the pack moulded to the curves of her back, spine, and hips.

'Is everyone comfortable?' Dallas asked.

'For now,' Eric said. 'Ask me again in an hour!'

Dallas grinned. 'You sound like an experienced hiker!'

Flora explained, 'Over the next two weeks, you'll find that you develop an interesting relation-ship with your backpack. You're totally dependent on it, you need it for survival, so you have to love it. But it will become a burden too, after you've been carrying it for long periods. As you tire, it will start feeling heavy, and it might rub you, making your back feel sore. That's when you're going to hate it.

It's going to take a while to get used to it, and sometimes you'll think of it as your worst enemy, but ultimately, you'll find that it's your best friend.'

Amy edged over to her real best friend. 'How does yours feel?' she asked.

'Okay,' Tasha said, but she was beginning to look nervous.

Amy whispered in her ear, 'If it gets too heavy for you, we'll figure out a way to transfer some of the stuff from your pack into mine. I can bear heavier weights than most people.'

Tasha managed a smile. 'Don't let everyone know that. You'll end up with six packs on your back.'

'Is everyone ready?' Flora asked.

The voices were uncertain, but they were unanimous. 'Yes.'

'Then we're off!' Dallas called. He led them away from the store, onto a wide path, and into the woods.

3

For the first hour of the hike, the trail was wide enough for the group to travel in a clump. But then the path narrowed, so they went two by two. And after half an hour they were walking in single file. Flora was at the head of the line; Dallas brought up the rear. Amy positioned herself behind Tasha, right in the middle, where her mother always told her she should be. Average people didn't attract attention.

But she seriously doubted that any members of the organisation were hiding in the trees, watching for clones. In fact, she felt unusually free and lighthearted as she walked along, with the bright sunlight peeking through the leafy boughs that hung above her. The air smelled clean and fresh; the weather was perfect, warm but not hot; and there was a nice breeze.

No one was saying much. Tasha looked over her shoulder. 'This reminds me of summer camp,' she said. 'Only I feel like we should be singing. You know, something like "Great Big Gobs of Greasy Grimy Gopher Guts," or "Ninety-nine Bottles of Beer on the Wall." '

'Maybe later,' Amy said, 'when we start feeling more comfortable together.' Personally, she didn't mind the lack of conversation at all. She liked hearing the crackle of the dead twigs under her feet, the soft rustle of the leaves, the birds. With no street sounds, no sirens or alarms or music blaring, she felt peaceful and completely at ease.

After a while, though, the crackling and rustling got to be a little boring, and the slow pace was making her restless. It turned out that Flora was into bird-watching, so every time she spotted an interesting bird she would tell Andy behind her, and he would pass the information down the line. But by the time Amy got the news, the bird had disappeared.

She twisted her neck to see Eric. 'How are your feet?' she asked. Eric had bought new hiking boots for this trip, and he'd spent the past week wearing them constantly to break them in.

'Okay,' he told her. 'At least, they're not hurting. Just dragging. I wish we could move a little faster.'

She peered towards the front of the line and reported back. 'I think it's Willard that's holding everyone up. He's slow.'

Minutes later the path widened again and they could break out of single file. Eric dropped back to talk to Dallas about the plans for their expedition. Tasha, in her warmhearted way, had taken pity on the morose, slow-moving Willard, and was trying to get him to open up and talk. Brooke and Flora were engrossed in a conversation, and Andy was just in front of them. Amy quickened her pace and caught up with Brooke and Flora.

They had apparently discovered a mutual interest in skiing. 'Have you tried the slopes on Mount Coral?' Brooke was asking Flora. 'The lines for the lifts are long, but it's worth the wait.'

'It's an awesome place,' Flora agreed. 'But there were too many kids on snowboards who didn't know what they were doing.'

'Oh, some of those snowboarders make me angry too,' Brooke agreed. 'There ought to be a law against them. They shouldn't be allowed on serious black diamond courses.'

Because she'd never skied in her life, there was no way Amy could join in the conversation, so she moved ahead of them and found herself alongside Andy. He smiled and said, 'I guess you're not into skiing.'

Amy shook her head. 'I'm from southern California. Cold weather doesn't do it for me.'

'I'm not too crazy about winter sports either. Give me summer sports and a blazing sun any day.'

'Do you play baseball?' Amy asked him.

'No. To tell you the truth, I'm not into team sports.'

'Same here,' Amy said. She lowered her voice. 'I hope I do okay on this expedition. The brochure said teamwork is very important.'

'I thought about that,' Andy admitted. 'I'm used to doing things on my own.'

'Me too,' Amy said.

They walked along in silence for a moment. 'Do you do any sports?' he asked.

'I like to swim,' Amy told him. 'And I used to do gymnastics.'

'Why did you stop?'

This was just the kind of question Amy hated – the kind she couldn't answer honestly. She couldn't tell Andy that she had been an outstanding gymnast, so talented that her coach had wanted her to compete. And that because of her talent her mother had made her quit. The last thing Amy needed was to display superior athletic skills on a national level.

But she had to respond to Andy's question. 'Well, gymnastics is very competitive, and—'

'And you're not into competition?' Andy looked at her with interest. 'Neither am I. For me, sports are fun. I don't have to win any medals.'

'Exactly,' Amy said in relief. She wasn't really in complete agreement. In fact, she loved to compete – but it put her life in too much danger.

'My father doesn't understand that,' Andy continued. 'He won a bunch of swimming medals when he was my age. I must be kind of a disappointment to him, being his only child.'

'I'm an only child too,' Amy said. 'It's not easy having all your parents' attention, is it?'

'No kidding. And I have just one parent. My mother died when I was a baby.'

'Really? I only have one parent too. My mother.'

'Did your father die?'

That was the story she and Nancy had always told people, so she nodded. 'I think that's even harder, when you're an only child,' she said. 'Your parent doesn't even have a partner to worry about.'

'So they concentrate all their worries on you,' Andy said.

'Exactly.' Amy exchanged a knowing smile with him. 'And I have to worry about *her*. Like, is she lonely when I'm not around?'

Andy nodded emphatically. 'And if they date, you have to worry about the people they go out with.'

'No kidding,' Amy said with feeling, recalling a certain man her mother had been seeing, who was more interested in kidnapping Amy than in dating Nancy. Once again, she and Andy shared an understanding smile.

'Hey, you two!' came a voice from way behind them. 'Slow down!'

They stopped walking and turned. A breathless Dallas was running towards them. 'Where's the fire?' he asked.

Amy realized that she couldn't even see the others behind him. Andy was surprised too. 'I didn't know we were moving so fast,' he said.

'You guys must be into racewalking,' Dallas grumbled. 'We're supposed to stay together.'

He was breathing hard, and his face was red with exertion. Dallas looked strong and healthy, but

Amy wondered if he really was in good shape. She and Andy hadn't been walking *that* fast. She was capable of moving at much greater speed, but if she had, Andy wouldn't have been able to keep pace with her. *No one* could have kept up with her. Except maybe another Amy.

'We'll wait here for the others,' she told Dallas. But her reluctance to do this must have shown on her face, because Dallas relented.

'Well, it's a straight path from here to the campsite,' he said. 'I guess it's okay for you guys to go on alone together.'

'Thanks,' Andy said, and they took off at a normal pace. 'He seems like a nice guy,' he remarked. 'I hope he isn't breaking some major rule letting us hike alone. I wouldn't want him to get into trouble, being a new counsellor and all.'

Amy thought it was nice of Andy to be concerned. 'He won't get into any trouble,' she assured Andy. 'Not with Flora, at least.'

'What makes you so sure?'

'The way they look at each other.' Amy could see that Andy still didn't understand what she meant. 'I'm pretty certain they're boyfriend and girlfriend.'

'Gee, I would never have guessed,' Andy said. 'Girls really are more sensitive to these things than guys.'

'Well, I don't know about that,' Amy demurred. 'Maybe it's just easier for us to *talk* about feelings. Because we're not into the macho thing.'

'Yeah, you're right,' Andy said. 'Guys are always trying to show how tough they are. I don't really understand it.' He grinned a little self-consciously. 'That's probably a dumb thing for me to say to a girl. Now you'll think I'm some kind of wimp.'

'No way,' Amy assured him. 'Girls like guys to be sensitive.' She was thinking of Eric as she spoke. He was usually pretty intuitive about other people's feelings. He just didn't like talking about them much. The only time he'd ever told her 'I love you' was when they both thought they were on the brink of extinction. And when the moment passed, he seemed to have forgotten the words.

'Look, that must be the campsite,' Andy said, pointing. They were entering a clearing where ropes and poles and canvases were spread out on the ground. 'Do you know how to pitch a tent?'

'No,' Amy said. 'But I'm a fast learner.' She watched as Andy demonstrated how to fit poles together and tie the canvas to the poles. Then she copied him.

'Be careful, those poles are pretty heavy,' Andy cautioned as she lifted one. Of course, it didn't feel particularly heavy at all, but Amy wondered if she should fake a little strain. She uttered a sigh, but Andy didn't notice. Then she decided she couldn't constantly worry about letting people see that she was strong. She wanted to relax and enjoy herself.

Dallas, Flora, and the others arrived at the clearing just as Amy and Andy finished pitching the fourth tent. 'Fast work,' Flora commented as she went around inspecting their work. 'And you guys did a nice job.'

Dallas looked impressed too, but he wasn't as complimentary. 'You should have waited until everyone got here, so we could pitch the tents together.'

'Not necessarily,' Flora said. 'Obviously, these two have had a lot of experience pitching tents. Teamwork doesn't always mean sharing the work. It means working for the good of the group.'

Dallas didn't say anything, but Amy got the feeling he didn't appreciate being contradicted.

He looked like the kind of person who was into that I'm-a-macho-guy attitude she and Andy had been talking about.

Flora looked up at the sky. 'Actually, I'm glad the tents are up. It took us longer to get here than I thought it would, and the sun's going down.'

Brooke looked pointedly at Willard and frowned. Eric frowned too, but not at Willard. He came over to Amy and pulled her aside.

'Are you nuts?' he demanded.

'What are you talking about?'

'Do you know how fast you were walking?'

Amy rolled her eyes. 'Oh, Eric, I couldn't have been moving *that* fast. Andy kept up with me.'

'Yeah, well, Andy's a guy, he's twice your size and at least three years older than you. You should have heard what the others were saying.'

'Like what?'

'Dallas said he'd never seen a girl walk that fast. Flora said you were in amazingly good shape for your age and size.'

Amy couldn't help preening a little, and Eric's frown deepened. 'This isn't a joke,' he said sternly. 'You know what your mother says. You don't want people talking about you.'

Amy raised an eyebrow. 'Since when did you start taking my mother's side?'

'Since she asked me to look out for you here,' he replied.

Now it was Amy's turn to frown. She was on the verge of reminding Eric that it was far more likely *she'd* be looking out for *him* than the other way around, but she held her tongue. She wouldn't call Eric macho, exactly, but he *was* a typical guy.

'Okay, okay,' she said, relenting. 'I'll try to be more careful.'

Tasha joined them. 'Do you see the platform someone built in that tree?' She pointed, and Amy looked. Actually, there were two platforms, one about twelve feet above the ground, the other a few feet lower. A rope ladder was hooked onto the higher platform and fell to the ground.

'What do you think that's for?' Tasha asked nervously.

'I don't have the slightest idea,' Amy replied. 'But I'm sure we'll find out. Hey, look at *that*.' She indicated a thick, long log that was lashed horizontally between two trees, about eight feet off the ground.

Now Tasha was looking a little sick. 'You don't think we have to walk on that log, do you?'

Amy tried to reassure her. 'Remember what Flora said? You don't have to do anything you don't want to do. But you should challenge yourself. Pretend you're on a balance beam. I'll even stay under the log to catch you if you fall.'

'That's exactly what you *shouldn't* do,' Eric warned her. 'Don't be a show-off!'

'Okay, okay,' Amy muttered. Was Eric going to be reminding her about this the entire week?

For the next half hour, they all went about the business of setting up camp. It turned out that the tents had been assigned in advance, and Amy was sharing with Brooke. Tasha didn't seem to mind. She was sharing a tent with Flora, and she liked the counsellor. Eric was sharing with Dallas, and Andy with Willard. Amy and Brooke went into their tent to unload their packs.

'What were you and Andy talking about when you were here by yourselves?' Brooke asked as she set a large flashlight down in a corner of the tent. Her tone was casual, but Amy wasn't fooled.

'Nothing too personal,' she assured her roomie. 'He's a nice guy.'

'Cute, too,' Brooke said, and Amy agreed.

'You know,' Brooke continued, 'this could work

out really well. You're with Eric, I'll be with Andy, and Tasha can have Willard.'

Amy seriously doubted that Tasha would go for that. She knelt down to roll out her sleeping bag, and her pendant caught the light from the lamp.

'That's pretty,' Brooke remarked. 'What is it? A moon?'

Amy nodded. 'A crescent moon. A friend of my family made it for me. He's dead now, so it's very special.'

'Then I'd take it off and put it away,' Brooke advised. 'You wouldn't want it falling off in the woods or on the river. You'd never find it.'

Amy smiled but made no move to remove the necklace. She never took it off. It had stayed with her through situations a lot more stressful than rock climbing and mountain biking were likely to be.

When they emerged from the tent, they saw that the rest of the group had already gathered around a fire. Flora was stirring the contents of a pot, and the aroma tickled Amy's nostrils. 'Mmm, chilli,' she commented.

'How can you tell from this far?' Brooke asked her.

Amy bit her lip. 'I, um, have a sharp sense of

smell.' It had never occurred to her before that her superiority in seeing and hearing extended to other senses – but why not? Happy to learn of another talent, she joined the others around the fire and accepted a warm bowl of chilli. Everyone looked tired and weary, but only Willard was complaining.

'My feet hurt,' he declared. 'How far did we hike today?'

Dallas was studying a map. 'Eleven kilometres,' he said. 'A kilometre is a little more than half a mile.'

'Point six two, to be exact,' Flora added. 'Which means, in miles we walked – does anyone have a pad and pencil? Or a calculator?'

'Six point eight two miles,' Amy said without thinking. The light from the fire was dim, but she didn't miss Eric's sharp look in her direction.

They finished their meal, which included roasted marshmallows, and there was talk of playing some word games, but most of them were too wiped out to think about anything but eating and sleeping. One by one they drifted off to their tents – first Tasha, then Brooke, then Eric and Willard.

Flora was stirring the fire, looking for sparks to extinguish, when Dallas turned to Amy. 'Are you some kind of maths whiz?' he asked pleasantly.

Amy wasn't sure how to reply, and fortunately she didn't have to because at that moment Andy let out a yelp. 'Wow, check out those stars!'

Amy looked up and couldn't help gasping. She'd never seen anything like this before. The sky was covered with clusters of tiny lights, like diamonds on a bed of dark blue velvet.

'This is something I love about getting out into the wilderness,' Andy said. 'You can't see a show of stars like this in a city.'

'It *is* nice,' Flora said. 'And when there's a full moon, it's truly spectacular.'

In the next few moments Andy went off to his tent, and Dallas followed soon after. Amy was getting pretty sleepy too, but she loved looking at the sky.

There was a crescent moon that night. Amy's hand automatically went to her pendant, and she fingered it.

'Amy, you'll want to take that off before we get really active,' Flora said. 'It could get caught on a bramble and break. Or even choke you. We don't wear any jewellery on Wilderness Adventure out-ings.'

That was her second warning. Amy sighed.

'Okay, I'll take it off.' She yawned. 'I guess I'd better hit the tent.'

'Sleep well,' Flora called out as she finished dousing the fire.

Brooke was already asleep when Amy crept into the tent, and it was pitch-black inside. She felt for the clasp behind her neck and opened it. She felt bare without her pendant, but it would be awful to lose it. She remembered what Dr Jaleski's daughter had told her when she gave Amy the necklace: 'He wanted you to have this, Amy, so you never forget who you are.'

Well, at least she still had the mark on her back – a crescent moon, identical in shape to the one that she now held in her hand. That would always be there. When the Amys were created, twelve years before, the mark was embedded in their skin, and it became visible when they reached puberty. Some kids at school who had seen it in the gym locker room thought it was a tattoo. Amy always told them it was a birthmark – which, in a way, was the truth.

She tucked the necklace into a pocket of her backpack, undressed, slipped on a nightgown, and crawled into her sleeping bag. She could feel herself dozing off when she heard a noise.

Her eyes jerked open. Was she imagining this? No, there was definitely a rustling sound just outside her tent.

She sat up, her heart pounding. Visions of big black bears crossed her mind . . . or were there mountain lions in this area? She'd never had to test her strength against an animal.

She wouldn't have to test it tonight. 'Amy!' a voice whispered. 'Are you awake?'

She crawled out of the bag and came out of the tent. 'Eric, what's wrong?'

'Nothing,' he told her. 'I just wanted to tell you . . .'

'Tell me what?' Was he going to suggest a romantic walk in the moonlight?

'Well, I didn't mean to snap at you about showing off. I promise I won't keep nagging you.'

'That's okay,' Amy told him. 'I know you're just looking out for me.'

'See you in the morning,' Eric said, and backed away.

''Night.' Amy blew him a kiss he probably couldn't see. She crept back into her tent and crawled into the sleeping bag. A moonlit walk would have been nice, but that wasn't really Eric's style.

4

After breakfast the next morning, the group was buzzing with anticipation as they waited to hear what their first real Wilderness Adventure experience would be. Amy figured she'd be able to get psyched up for just about anything, but she was hoping the challenge of the day would be hang-gliding.

She was always reminding Eric and Tasha that despite her extraordinary strength and other unusual physical skills, she was no superhero. And there *was* nothing magical about her abilities. She couldn't read minds or predict futures. She couldn't change history, and she couldn't fly. She could only do what any human being could do, only far better. But sometimes, in her own private fantasies, she wished she could soar through the sky, sailing over snow-capped mountains, up, up, up into the clouds . . .

But she doubted that their group would be thrown into something as dramatic as hang-gliding so soon. And poor Tasha was definitely not ready for something that daring. Amy really didn't care what they did today. Whatever it was would be exciting.

Or maybe not. Flora dashed any hopes Amy held for a thrilling experience when she announced that the day would be devoted to exercises. Then she laughed at the groans of dismay that greeted her announcement.

'We're not talking about sit-ups and jumping jacks,' she told them. 'These are exercises designed to prepare you for the adventures to come, and we think you'll find them very interesting.'

'If you survive them,' Dallas added with a wicked grin. A nervous titter passed through the group.

Flora smiled, but she gave Dallas a look of mild rebuke. 'Let's not scare them,' she said. 'Really, guys, there's nothing to worry about. We're not testing you as athletes. Today we're more concerned with establishing a sense of community and an ability to relate to each other as a team. And the most important aspect of relating to each other is trust. Before Dallas and I lead you into challenging situations, we need to know that you can trust each other.'

Amy wasn't quite sure what Flora was talking about. Trust each other for what? She looked around and realised the others were doing the same. Nobody appeared too confident.

'Now,' Flora continued, 'I trust Dallas completely.' She walked over to where Dallas was standing and positioned her back in front of him. 'I trust him so much that I'm going to let myself fall, because I know he'll catch me before I hit the ground.' She stood very stiffly, with her arms by her sides. And then, slowly, she let herself fall backwards.

Dallas caught her. The group looked at each other, not sure how to respond. After all, what Flora and Dallas had done didn't look all that difficult.

'Now, who would like to volunteer to take my place?' Flora asked. 'Who trusts Dallas as much as I do?'

Tasha edged over by Amy. 'That's easy enough for her to say,' she muttered. 'He's her boyfriend; he's not going to let her smash *her* head on the ground.'

Brooke apparently felt that Dallas would do the same for her. She stepped forward and assumed Flora's position, standing stiffly with her back in front of Dallas. But as Brooke let her body go, she moved an arm to break her fall – just in case Dallas missed.

Dallas caught her, of course, but Flora made it clear that Brooke hadn't performed the exercise properly. 'When you put an arm back like that,' she told Brooke, 'you're saying you don't completely trust Dallas to catch you. What we're asking you to do is to put your well-being completely in another person's hands. Okay? Everybody up.'

She paired them off – Brooke with Willard, Amy with Andy, Tasha with Eric. Amy could hear Tasha sigh with relief. She and her brother might argue a lot and get on each other's nerves, but she was obviously confident he wouldn't want her head smashed on the ground.

Amy felt confident too. She didn't know Andy the way Tasha knew Eric, but their conversation the day before had made her feel comfortable. Now, if she could just manage not to let her instinctive desire to take care of herself force her arm back in a defensive move.

Like Tasha and Brooke, she stood stiffly. 'Are you ready?' Flora asked. 'One, two, three, fall!'

It wasn't easy, but Amy resisted making an effort to break her fall. She certainly wasn't accustomed to feeling helpless, and for an instant, as she fell, she experienced actual panic, as intense as any fear she'd ever felt in much more dangerous circumstances. So the relief she experienced when Andy's strong arms gripped her was just as important as the way she felt whenever she realised she was out of danger. Except that she usually got *herself* out of danger. It was strange, relying on someone else.

Then they switched positions, with the girls catching the boys. Willard was alarmed. 'Brooke's smaller than I am,' he complained. 'She'll drop me.'

'She won't have to bear your whole weight,' Flora explained. 'She's just breaking your fall.'

'But how do I know she'll do that?'

'You have to trust her,' Flora said patiently. 'That's the point of the exercise.'

Amy and Andy exchanged smiles. It was becoming clear that Willard would be a whiner. 'Don't worry,' Amy told Andy. 'I'll catch you.'

'I know you will,' Andy said simply.

It was nice, the way he said that – as if he really,

honestly trusted her. And when he did fall stiffly, without the slightest effort to help himself, she felt there was now a bond between them. After that, they all switched partners, twice more, so that each person had the opportunity to catch and be caught by everyone there. Amy had no worries when it came to Tasha or Eric, but she *did* experience a tiny bit of nervousness when paired with Willard and Brooke. They both caught her, but she couldn't really say she felt any particular bond with them once the exercise was completed.

Next, Flora and Dallas directed them to the log lashed between the two trees that Amy had noticed the day before. It was about eight feet off the ground, a foot in diameter, and Amy guessed it was around twelve feet long. Tasha had been afraid they'd have to walk across it, but that wasn't the exercise.

'This is a test of teamwork,' Flora told them. 'The object is to get the entire group over the log to the other side.'

Willard went under the log and raised his arms. 'It's impossible,' he declared. 'I'm the tallest one here and I can't reach the log.'

'There *is* a way to do it,' Flora said. 'But that's all

I'll say. You have to figure out how.' She and Dallas walked a few yards away, where they sat on a large rock and watched them.

The six campers drew in closer. Silently they all looked at their obstacle. 'Could we climb the trees?' Brooke wondered aloud.

Andy moved closer and investigated. 'No,' he told them, 'there are no limbs low enough to grip.'

'Maybe we could vault over the log,' Eric suggested. 'We could find a sturdy stick to use as a pole.'

'That won't work,' Amy declared. 'Even if we knew how to pole vault, there's nothing on the other side to break our falls. We'd kill ourselves.'

'It was just an idea,' Eric muttered, and Amy wondered if she'd spoken too bluntly.

'There must be broken logs around here,' Tasha said. 'Why don't we gather some, along with rocks, and pile them up? We could climb the pile and get over that way.'

It was an interesting proposition, but before they could act on it, Flora called out to them. 'I forgot to tell you: you can't use anything except your own bodies. No ladders, no ropes, no equipment. But you can use Dallas and me.'

Again the group fell silent as they contemplated the challenge before them. Then Amy had an idea.

It wasn't a completely original notion. In fact, it was based on Tasha's suggestion that they build a pile that could be climbed – but they'd use their own bodies instead of logs and rocks. She played it out in her mind and realised that yes, it could work – but she hesitated to propose it. It wasn't just her superior physical strength that needed to be kept in check, but also her ability to think more quickly than other people.

'How about this?' Andy said slowly. 'We could climb on each other.'

'What do you mean?' Eric asked.

'We make a human pyramid,' Andy explained. 'Four people stand on the ground. Two people get on their shoulders. The remaining two climb them and get onto the log. Then the two on the log reach down and help pull the others up.'

Amy drew her breath in sharply. It was amazing – that was exactly the idea *she'd* had! Maybe she wasn't so brilliant after all.

They discussed the possibilities and came up with a pyramid configuration based on size and weight.

Andy called Flora and Dallas over and organised the structure.

Dallas, Willard, Flora, and Eric were positioned under the log. Eric and Flora bent down so Amy could put one foot on each of their shoulders, while Dallas and Willard did the same for Tasha. Brooke and Andy climbed the human pyramid, which put them in easy reach of the log. Wrapping their legs around the log, they sat on it, and then reached down for Amy. Between them, they were able to pull her up.

'Now what?' Amy asked as she straddled the log.

'How do you feel about jumping down from here?' Andy asked her.

It was only eight feet, but that was far enough to cause damage to someone who landed wrong. Amy didn't have to worry about that, though. 'No problem,' she said, slipping off the log and landing squarely on her feet on the other side.

Tasha wasn't able to do it quite so easily. Brooke and Andy got her hands, but she had to kick and thrash to get herself onto the log. And she didn't feel very good about jumping down the other side.

'I'll break your fall,' Amy promised her.

That didn't placate Tasha. 'Can you catch me?' she asked in a panic.

Amy wasn't sure what to say. Of course she *could* catch Tasha – she was physically capable of having Tasha's weight fall on her without getting knocked over. But she'd be showing off her physical abilities – and what would the others think?

She wanted to tell Tasha she'd be fine, but Tasha looked so frightened . . .

'Okay,' Amy said, relenting. 'I'll catch you.'

Tasha squeezed her eyes shut and let herself drop. Amy caught her in her arms and quickly lowered her to the ground, hoping that she had moved so fast no one would think twice about it. And it seemed that she had succeeded – at least, no one said anything. For a fleeting second, though, she thought Dallas looked at her oddly.

Then Willard got onto Dallas's shoulders while Flora balanced on Eric's. Andy and Brooke reached down, grabbed them one at a time, and got them over. Finally Eric got on Dallas's shoulders, and was able to get on and over the log without too much trouble.

'What about me?' Dallas asked. 'Remember, you have to get *everyone* over the log.'

That was a problem. But once again, Andy came up with a solution. He conferred with Brooke. Then, slowly, they both moved around on the log, and bent forward at stomach level over it. 'Grab our wrists,' Andy told Dallas. 'We'll hoist you up.'

Looking doubtful, Dallas did as he was told. But he was rising lopsided – Brooke just didn't have the strength to pull him up.

Eric had an idea. 'I'll get back up and take Brooke's place,' he called out.

'No,' Andy yelled back. 'I can do it. Dallas, let go of Brooke and take my other wrist.' And to everyone's amazement, Andy was able to hoist Dallas off the ground, high enough so that Dallas grabbed the log and swung himself over onto the other side. Then Andy and Brooke dropped down, with the others breaking their fall.

A cheer went up from the group. 'We did it! We did it!' everyone shrieked.

Brooke gazed at Andy with utter awe. 'You are so strong!'

Flora too was very impressed. 'I've never seen it done quite that way before,' she said.

'Yeah,' Dallas said, looking at Andy thoughtfully. 'Pretty amazing.'

Andy blushed slightly. 'I work out,' he mumbled.

They went on to the next exercise. Tasha had wondered about the two platforms built into the tree, with the rope ladder hanging down from the higher one. Now they learned how the platforms were to be used.

'Each of you will climb the ladder to the higher platform,' Flora told them. 'From there you'll jump down to the lower one.'

That didn't seem like much of a test to Amy. The platforms weren't far apart, so the jump wouldn't be difficult. Even Tasha didn't look particularly unnerved.

'How would you like to go first?' Dallas asked her with a smile.

Tasha's face went pink. 'Okay.' She climbed the rope ladder to the higher platform.

'Ready to jump?' Flora called out.

But Tasha didn't move. She just stood there, frozen, looking down.

'Go on,' Dallas called. 'Jump!'

Amy wondered who else saw the fear on Tasha's face.

'Jump, jump, jump,' the other campers began to call out in unison. But Tasha didn't – or couldn't –

move. She backed away from the edge of the platform, slowly, inch by inch, knelt, and grabbed the edges of the rope ladder. Trembling, she made her way back down.

'What's the matter?' Brooke demanded. Tasha didn't reply. She walked rapidly away from the group, and Amy wasn't sure if she was the only one who could hear her crying.

Immediately, Amy took a step to go after her friend, but Flora touched her arm. 'Let Dallas talk to her,' she murmured. Amy watched as Dallas caught up to Tasha, put his arm around her shoulder, and began speaking quietly with her.

'Why don't you go next, Amy?' Flora suggested.

Amy glanced uncertainly at Tasha, but her friend seemed to be getting calmer as she listened to whatever Dallas was saying. 'Okay,' she said, and climbed the rope ladder.

Once she was on the upper platform, she could see why Tasha had freaked. Standing on the ground, looking up, it hadn't seemed like a big deal at all. But now, on the perch, looking down, the lower platform seemed to have shrunk. It was tiny, maybe two feet square, and it looked very far away. And very easy to miss.

Even Amy felt her heartbeat quicken. She was a lot higher here than she'd been on the log. But she took a deep breath, focused, and leaped.

She made it, landing neatly on the lower platform, and realised that the appearance of the test was scarier than the reality. But as she watched the others take their turn, she saw how their expressions changed when they eyed the lower platform from the higher one. Poor Willard was really nervous. When he hit the target, he fell into a crouch and grasped the edges of the platform with both hands, as if afraid he'd topple off.

Eric was next, and Amy wanted to give him some tips. 'Keep your arms out to the sides, not too close to your body,' she told him. 'That way you get more balance and you won't wobble like Willard.'

But Eric didn't welcome her advice. 'Are you comparing me with *him*?' he asked.

'No, I'm just telling you how to do the leap better.'

'I think I can figure that out for myself.'

Why was Eric acting like that? Amy wondered. Was it that macho thing?

Finally everyone had completed the task – except for Tasha. But when she returned to the group, with Dallas, she announced in a quivering voice that she was ready to try it again. She climbed the ladder and stood on the platform. Amy could still see fear on her face. But somehow Tasha found the courage to leap. And she made it down to the second platform safely.

Everyone cheered. Tasha was still shaking when she reached the ground, but there was no mistaking the pride on her face. Amy rushed over and hugged her.

'That was great!' she told her. 'Congratulations!'

Tasha's eyes were shining. 'It was Dallas. He talked me into it. He's so wonderful!'

'No, *you're* wonderful,' Amy insisted. '*You* did it!'

But it was soon clear that Tasha was now in – well, not in love, but definitely in awe. She gazed at Dallas in total adoration. As they all moved on to the next exercise, she skipped ahead to walk alongside him. Amy looked at Flora, who smiled and shook her head ruefully.

'Dallas is very good with the girls,' she told Amy. 'They all adore him, and they want to do their best for him.'

'I guess that's good,' Amy said.

Flora shook her head. 'It's much better if they

want to do their best for themselves, for their own self-esteem. Not that I'm not glad Dallas helped Tasha, but she shouldn't do something simply because she thinks he'll like her better.'

Amy understood what Flora was saying. She made a mental note to talk about it with Tasha later.

The next exercise took place at a large boulder. 'We're going to do some practise climbing now,' Flora told them, 'to get ready for some real rock climbing tomorrow.'

'I thought tomorrow was white-water rafting,' Eric said.

'Well, that's the plan now,' Flora said, gazing up at the cloudy sky. 'But it looks like it might rain tonight, and the water may be too high tomorrow. We'll have to wait and see. Meanwhile, let's work on climbing and belaying.'

'Be-whatting?' Willard asked, wearing that look of trepidation they were all becoming familiar with.

Dallas produced the climbing rope and explained how the climber tied one end of the rope around his waist, while the belayer stood at the top of the rock, taking the rope in and keeping the climber from slipping off. The two counsellors demonstrated, with Flora on top of the boulder, and Dallas going down and around to the ledge below, before climbing back up.

When it was Amy's turn to climb, she realised how important the role of the belayer was. In her pairing, it was Willard who was holding the rope taut – or at least, that was what he was supposed to be doing. He wasn't putting much energy into his effort, and the rope kept going slack. Amy was able to cling to the rocks, but Willard wasn't providing any assistance.

Fortunately, Flora was up on top of the boulder with him, and she pointed out what he was doing wrong. Amy used the rope to help herself get up the vertical rock ledge.

When it was Amy's turn to act as belayer, she found herself next to Eric. She tried belaying first, holding the rope taut so Brooke could climb the boulder. Then it was Eric's turn to hold the rope for Willard.

'Better keep it taut,' Amy said to him. 'Willard doesn't have much of a grip.'

'I *know* that,' Eric murmured. Even so, Willard wasn't making much progress up the boulder.

'I feel like I'm going to slip off,' Willard called out.

Eric was getting annoyed. 'You're not going to slip off,' he yelled back. 'Just hold on.'

'The rope feels loose,' Willard complained.

Amy examined Eric's hold on the rope. 'You know, if you turn your wrist, you can get a tighter hold on it,' she told him.

'Since when are you the authority on belaying?' Eric snapped.

'I'm just trying to help.'

'Yeah, well, I know you can do everything better than me,' Eric said through his teeth. 'But you don't have to point that out to everyone!'

Amy rolled her eyes. 'Sorry.' What's got into him? she wondered. He was always so proud of her skills.

'I'm falling!' Willard shrieked.

Amy grabbed the rope and began pulling. 'Hey!' Eric barked. 'I've got it!' And with his elbow, he practically shoved Amy aside.

Amy was shocked. 'Eric!' she yelled. But Eric was concentrating on getting Willard up the boulder and ignored her. For once in her life, Amy felt utterly helpless and confused.

5

In the tent that evening, Brooke couldn't stop talking about Andy. 'Did you *see* how he lifted Dallas? I could tell he has a great body, but I had no idea he was *that* strong! And it's not like Dallas is some puny little thing. It was like watching trapeze flyers in a circus. And he's really intelligent, too. I would never have thought of making a human pyramid.'

Amy made a noise to indicate she was listening as she slipped a nightgown over her head. She'd been impressed with Andy too, but right now her thoughts were elsewhere.

'I wonder if he has a girlfriend,' Brooke continued. 'He doesn't live that far from me, you know. Sometimes I go to San Francisco for weekends and stay with a girl-friend there.'

'Mmm,' Amy acknowledged as she crawled into her sleeping bag. She hoped Brooke wasn't going to prattle all night. It had been a long and active day, and she was wiped out.

Fortunately, after a few more comments about Andy's good looks and gorgeous blue eyes, Brooke ran out of compliments, and soon after that her slow, even breathing told Amy she was asleep.

But as tired as Amy was, she couldn't sleep. Behind the lids of her closed eyes, she kept seeing Eric's angry expression. She was still puzzled by his reaction. He'd easily accepted the fact that she was better at doing just about anything than he was, and he'd never been jealous of her talents. And she hadn't been showing off in a way that could put her in danger, so why had he been upset with her? It had to be something else . . .

Amy knew she wouldn't be able to sleep until she had some answers. Crawling out of her sleeping bag, she wrapped a sweater around her shoulders and crept silently out of the tent.

The tent that Eric was sharing with Dallas was diagonally across the clearing. She moved carefully around the area where the fire had been burning, just in case there were still some hot patches. She wasn't quite sure how to signal Eric without alerting Dallas, and debated a few possibilities before realising she didn't have to worry about waking either of them. They weren't sleeping. She was still about five yards from the tent when she picked up their whispered conversation. Stopping, she remembered she'd made a pledge to herself to quit eavesdropping on private conversations. As tempting as it was, she knew it wasn't right to use her superior hearing to invade other people's conversations. *Whatever they're talking about, it's none of your business*, she warned herself. How would she like it if Eric spied on her?

But then she heard her name. And as virtuous as she wanted to be, she was only human – sort of. So, with some effort, she tuned out her conscience and focused her hearing in the direction of the voices.

Dallas was speaking. 'So she's your girlfriend, right?'

'Yeah.'

'She's a pretty tough character, huh?'

'What do you mean?'

'She strikes me as someone who's pretty sure of herself. And she's strong for her size.'

Amy could barely make out Eric's murmur of

assent, but she wasn't worried. She knew Eric would never tell Dallas why she was so strong. That was one thing she could be totally sure of – Eric's loyalty. Even if he was angry at her, he would never betray her.

'Smart, too,' Dallas continued. 'I couldn't believe how fast she calculated that maths in her head. Is she some kind of genius?'

'No,' Eric said quickly. 'She's just good in maths. Makes all A's.'

'Must be hard on you,' Dallas said.

Either Eric didn't reply, or he spoke so softly that even her ears couldn't pick it up.

'I know what it's like,' Dallas continued. 'Having a girlfriend who acts like she's in charge is rough on a guy's ego. Especially around other people.'

This time she didn't miss Eric's mumbled 'Yeah.'

So *that* was it. Eric hadn't suddenly decided that her abilities were obnoxious. He just didn't want others to know that she was stronger, smarter, and better at everything than he was. She shook her head wearily. *Boys.*

Well, she had her answer. She could go back to her own tent now and think about what she should do to make Eric feel better. But she couldn't resist lingering another moment as Dallas spoke again.

'Let me give you some advice, Eric. You can't let a girlfriend get too full of herself. Believe me, I know. Flora orders me around because she's got seniority in this organisation. But I really don't appreciate her embarrassing me in front of the campers.'

Amy was a little startled to hear this. She wasn't surprised – after all, she'd noticed the dark looks Dallas occasionally shot in Flora's direction. But she did think it was odd for him to be telling Eric his feelings so forthrightly. They must be getting pretty palsy-walsy, she decided. She just hoped Dallas's massive macho attitude wouldn't rub off on Eric.

But now she had to think about how she was going to deal with Eric's feelings. She could apologise, but she wasn't sure if that would help or simply remind him that she would always be better than he was. Maybe she should just keep her opinions to herself for a while . . .

She was lost in thought, and the faint humming sound didn't register right away. When it did, she stopped and looked around. It was a human voice, and it was coming from the direction of the boulder they'd climbed earlier. She hoped it was Flora, and it occurred to her that she wouldn't mind a heart-to-heart talk about boys with an older, more experienced woman right about now.

She made her way down the trail to the boulder, and when the tree branches split off to reveal the big rock, she saw right away that it wasn't Flora. It was Andy.

She watched him for a while as he stared up at the sky, humming softly. Then he looked in her direction, with a smile on his face. Once again, she felt the bond they seemed to have established that day. And his smile was magnetic. She made her way farther down the path and over to him.

He didn't seem all that surprised to see her. 'Hi. You couldn't sleep either?'

Amy nodded. 'What are you doing?'

He gave her a slightly abashed grin. 'Stargazing. I guess it's kind of a hobby of mine.'

'Really? Do you have a telescope at home?'

'No, I'm not that serious. I just like picking out the constellations. Do you ever do that?'

'I went to a planetarium once on a class trip,' Amy said. 'But to tell you the truth, I didn't have much luck picking out any designs in the sky. It reminded me of those connect-the-dots games you play when you're little. Only I couldn't use a pencil, so it was just a mess of dots for me!'

Andy laughed. 'Come on up and I'll connect them for you.'

She climbed up the boulder, and Andy edged over on the flat surface to make room for her. 'You've heard of the Big Dipper, right?' he asked her.

'Sure.'

'Okay, look over there. There are seven really bright stars – can you see them?'

'Yes.'

'They make the shape of a dipper. Three of them form the handle, and four make the bowl.'

'Oh.' Amy tried mentally to block out all the other stars around them and see the shape of a dipper. 'Yeah! I can make it out.'

'And there's the Little Dipper, to the left of it,' Andy went on. 'Now, that mess of stars over there, that's Orion, and you can make out Orion's Belt. And those five stars that make the shape of a *W*, that's called Cassiopeia.'

She was amazed to find that she could actually make out the patterns he was describing. 'Wow, this is cool!'

'And over there, that's my favourite. It's called the Seven Sisters.'

Amy counted the stars in the group. 'One, two, three, four, five, six, seven – I get it!'

He turned to her. 'You see all seven?'

'Sure. Why?'

'Most people can only see six of the Seven Sisters,' he told her.

'Well . . . I have good eyesight.'

'Yeah, me too. You know what's interesting? The constellation patterns we see in the sky aren't real at all. I mean, the way we see stars from Earth is different from the way they're actually arranged in space.'

'Is it possible to see how they're actually arranged?' Amy asked him.

'I don't think so,' he said. 'Not even with good eyesight.'

They fell silent for a few moments, looking up and contemplating the lights. Then Andy spoke. 'What did you think of those exercises today?'

'They were okay,' Amy said. 'That trust fall, or whatever they call it, was kind of weird.'

'Yeah, I know what you mean,' Andy agreed. 'Especially when I had to let Willard catch me. He looked so nervous, for a second I thought he was afraid to stick his arms out!'

Amy laughed. She'd had the same thought.

'And I was a little worried about your friend, Tasha,' he went on. 'She's kind of small. I was afraid I might knock her down.'

'She's stronger than she looks,' Amy assured him.

'So are you,' he commented. 'But I wasn't worried about hitting the ground when I knew you were behind me. I knew you'd catch me.'

'Oh yeah?' Amy punched his shoulder playfully. 'What made you so sure of that?'

'Because I trust you,' he said simply. 'I don't know why, I just sort of feel like, well, like I know you. Like we're already friends or something.'

Amy wasn't sure how to respond. She surprised herself when she blurted out, 'I have the same feeling about you.'

'Really?'

'Yeah, like we've met before. Which we haven't, I'm sure. I'd remember you.' She paused. 'Maybe we have this feeling because we talked on the hike to the clearing.'

'Maybe,' he echoed, though he didn't sound convinced.

They sat in silence again for a moment, and it was a comfortable silence. Still, Amy felt a little peculiar about being out here alone with a guy she barely knew, even if he didn't feel like a stranger. So she got the conversation going again.

'You were good at belaying this afternoon. Better than anyone else.'

'Thanks,' he replied. 'I've had a little experience. My father and I go rock climbing now and then.'

'You're close to him, huh?'

'Yeah,' he said. 'Even though we're complete opposites. I swear, sometimes we look at each other like we're from different planets.'

Amy laughed. 'I get those looks from my mother, too, and I give them right back to her. Most everyone I know thinks that at least one of their parents is an alien.'

'It's different for me, though,' Andy said. 'I was adopted. So it's not like my father and I are related by blood.'

That was interesting. In a way, *Amy* was adopted too. At least, she had no blood connection to her mother. She couldn't mention this, though. It was the kind of comment that could bring up questions.

Like the questions she wanted to ask Andy right now.

'Do you know anything about your birth parents?'

'No, nothing.'

'I saw a TV movie once, about an adopted girl who searched for her birth mother. Have you ever thought about doing that?'

'Not really.'

'Aren't you the least bit curious?'

'No.'

Suddenly she was embarrassed by all her questions. She was coming across as awfully nosy. Did he want her to leave him alone now?

Apparently not, because he asked the next question. 'That guy Eric . . . he's Tasha's brother, right?'

'Right,' she replied.

After a second, he added, 'And your boyfriend. Right?'

'Yes.' The word came out stronger than she'd intended it to. He looked at her with naked interest.

'He doesn't act like a boyfriend,' he said bluntly. Then, when Amy didn't reply immediately, he said, 'Sorry, that's none of my business.'

'It's okay,' she said automatically.

'I couldn't help overhearing the way he was talking to you,' Andy said. 'When you were showing him how to hold the rope.'

Amy shrugged. 'I think he was just embarrassed because I corrected him in public. The macho guy thing. *You* know.'

'No,' Andy said. 'I don't. What's his problem, anyway?'

'He doesn't have any problem,' she said quickly, feeling disloyal for even talking about Eric with Andy.

'If I were your boyfriend, I wouldn't talk to you like that.'

She felt like she ought to give him a flippant response, something like, 'Well, you're not my boyfriend.' But for some reason she couldn't bring herself to say anything at all.

'Andy? Andy, is that you?' The eager voice came from below them. Amy looked down and saw Brooke standing there.

'Yeah, it's me,' Andy answered.

'And me,' Amy said.

Brooke's voice went through a subtle change. 'Oh. Hi, Amy. What are you guys up to?'

'Just looking at the stars,' Andy said.

Amy tried to counter the romantic image those words conveyed. 'Are you into astronomy, Brooke? Andy knows all the constellations. He's been showing me how to identify them. We can see the Seven Sisters.'

'Sure you can,' Brooke said, and there was no mistaking the sarcasm in her voice.

And then a beam of harsh light hit Amy square in the face. 'Brooke! Turn off that flashlight!'

But it wasn't Brooke who had the flashlight. 'What are you guys doing up there?' Dallas was coming toward them, aiming his flashlight directly at their faces.

'Just talking,' Andy said.

'Well, you should all be in your tents.' Dallas looked from one to the other. 'You've got a busy day tomorrow, and you need your sleep. Besides, it's about to rain.' He made no attempt to hide the annoyance in his voice. 'And you know, we have some rules here at Wilderness Adventure. No fooling around. That's why we separate the boys and the girls in different tents.'

Amy looked down from the rock and glared at Dallas. 'We were *not* fooling around,' she stated with as much dignity as she could muster. 'If you must know, we were stargazing. The Big Dipper and all that.'

'Yeah, right.' Dallas snorted. 'With those clouds, you can barely see the moon.' As if to confirm his statement, a low rumble of thunder came from above them, and then a streak of lightning crossed the skies. Less than a second later, the first few drops began to fall.

Amy and Andy scrambled down from the rock, and they all took off in the direction of the camp. Amy got into her tent just ahead of Brooke.

'Yikes, I'm soaked,' Amy commented. She picked up a towel for herself and threw another one to Brooke.

'What were you two *really* doing on that rock?' Brooke wanted to know.

'Just looking at stars,' Amy insisted. 'And talking. We were *not* fooling around.'

Brooke sniffed. 'Well, I should hope not. I thought you had a boyfriend.'

'I do,' Amy said as she crawled back into her sleeping bag.

At least, she *thought* she did.

6

Amy met Tasha the next morning by the stream, where they washed and brushed their teeth. The rain from the night before had made the bank muddy. Clad in her bathing suit, Tasha stepped gingerly into the stream and made a face.

'Is it cold?' Amy asked her.

'No. It's just that I keep expecting to step on something icky.' Tasha sighed. 'You know what I like about my bathtub at home? No fish.'

Amy strode into the water with her bar of soap. 'I think it feels neat to take a bath outside. It's like we're back in the Stone Age or something.'

'I'll take civilisation any day, thank you,' Tasha replied.

'Oh, come on, Tasha, you're enjoying this just a little bit, aren't you?'

'It's okay, I guess,' Tasha said. 'What are we doing today?'

'Rafting, I think. Remember that picture in the brochure?'

'I remember,' Tasha said, and her tone made it clear that it wasn't a particularly pleasant memory. 'It looked scary.'

'Exciting,' Amy corrected her. 'You'll love it.'

'Only if you're in the same raft with me,' Tasha said.

'I don't know how they'll divide us up,' Amy replied.

'Amy, *please* be in the same raft with me,' Tasha begged. 'Make a fuss about it. Tell them I'll have a panic attack, or worse, a total and complete mental breakdown.'

'A mental breakdown? Isn't that a little extreme?'

'Not necessarily,' Tasha said. 'Okay, maybe I won't have a breakdown. But if we're bouncing around on water, I'll definitely get motion sickness. Isn't that bad enough?'

Amy burst out laughing. 'Oh, that's just great. You want us to be together so you can throw up all over *me*.'

'Well, I'd rather throw up on you than a total stranger.'

'Like Dallas?' Amy asked with a knowing wink.

Tasha turned bright pink. 'Ohmigosh, what if I *did* throw up in front of him? I'd just *die*.'

'Don't tell me you've fallen madly in love with Dallas,' Amy said. 'Isn't he a little old for you?'

'I can have fantasies, can't I?' Tasha retorted. 'Don't you think he's sexy?'

'Not really,' Amy replied honestly. Her recollection of his tone when he found her and Andy on the rock the night before had sent him way down in her esteem.

Tasha wasn't offended by her opinion. 'I guess that's what happens when you have a real-life boyfriend. You stop thinking other guys are sexy.'

Amy couldn't come up with an immediate response to that.

'Of course, I really wouldn't mind being in the same raft as Dallas,' Tasha said. 'If I fell into the river, he could jump in and rescue me.' She shivered in imagined delight.

But it appeared that they wouldn't be going out on rafts that day. 'It was a heavy rain last night,' Flora told them all at breakfast. 'The water's too high. It's over the acceptable level for rafting.' She put up a hand to ward off the groans of the campers. 'We'll do some real rock climbing instead,' she told them. 'And by the day after tomorrow, if it doesn't rain again, the water will be down to a level where we can take the rafts out.'

'Wait a minute,' Dallas said. 'The water's only slightly over the level. I don't see why we can't go rafting today. It can't make that much of a difference. *I've* rafted on waters higher than this with no problem.'

The briefest frown crossed Flora's face, but she replied calmly. 'Yes, I've rafted on high waters too, but this is the rule. The water's at two point five, and the highest allowable level for Wilderness Adventure programmes is two point three.'

'Oh, come on,' Dallas remonstrated. 'Two point three, two point five, that's nitpicking.'

'Yeah,' Eric said. 'Why can't we bend the rules a little? *I* don't care if the water is two-tenths of a point higher than it's supposed to be. What about the rest of you?'

Andy and Brooke both made noises that indicated their willingness to go on the water. But Flora still shook her head.

'Sorry, guys,' she began, but before she could say

any more, Dallas took her arm. They walked away
from the campfire to avoid being overheard. Of
course, they didn't know they had a pair of super
ears in their midst. Amy tuned in.

'This is stupid,' Dallas was saying. 'You're going
to throw us completely off schedule. The hang-
gliding equipment arrives on Tuesday, remember?
Besides, if it rains tonight, the river will really be too
high, and it won't go down enough before the
week is over.'

'But Dallas—'

'Look, you may be the counsellor with seniority,
but I'm more experienced with white-water rafting
than you are. Remember that vacation we took in
Colorado? Remember how I handled the rapids?
Are you going to tell me that you know more about
rafting than I do?'

Amy couldn't see the counsellors, but she sus-
pected that Flora was torn between following
regulations and not wanting to injure Dallas's macho pride. Amy understood. She glanced at Eric,
and he looked at her. Then he looked away.

Caught up in her own thoughts, she didn't listen
to the rest of Flora and Dallas's conversation. But
apparently Flora had given in, because when they

returned to the group she announced that they would be rafting after all.

When they reached the river, Amy had to admit that the water certainly didn't look dangerous. It was smooth as silk, clear and calm. Dallas set to work inflating the rafts while Flora distributed bright orange life jackets.

Eric objected. 'Do we have to wear these things? Look at the water! You'd have to be weighted down with cement to drown in it!'

'Sorry,' Flora said lightly. 'Rules and regulations, you know. And the water can get rougher downstream.'

Amy saw Eric exchange a look with Dallas. Personally, she was getting a little bothered by the counsellor's influence on him. Somehow, she had to find an opportunity to talk with Eric privately.

Before they could get into the rafts, they were given instructions. Flora demonstrated what to do if they were flipped out of the raft. 'You'll want to swim on your back, with your feet pointing downstream to fend off rocks. Dallas, would you show them the correct way to handle the paddles?'

Dallas held a paddle up for them to see. 'This is

the regular stroke,' he said, demonstrating the movement. 'When you have to get around an obstacle, you pull the oar through the water like this, against the current. Now, you don't want the paddle knocked out of your hands, because once it's floating in the water it won't be easy to retrieve, particularly when there's current. So you need to grip it firmly, with both hands, and—'

'Dallas,' Flora interrupted. 'There should be more space between each hand. That way you have more control.'

A shadow crossed Dallas's face, but either Flora didn't notice or she chose not to. Quickly, she divided them into two groups, and Tasha was in luck. She had both Amy and Dallas in the raft with her. Eric was with them too. Without discussing the subject, the boys took the front seats, while Tasha and Amy got in the back. Amy was annoyed at the way the guys just assumed they would be in the lead, but she kept her feelings to herself. She didn't want any more problems with Eric, especially not in front of his new role model.

So she settled back, determined to enjoy herself. The sun was shining, the air was fresh, and she was here to have fun. This wasn't like the picture in the

Wilderness Adventure brochure, though. The rafts weren't moving fast – no one was paddling furiously. Amy felt like her raft was moving in slow motion.

The other raft floated along just a few feet from them, and she smiled at Andy, who was sitting alongside Brooke behind Flora and Willard. Obviously, *Andy* didn't feel it was necessary to be in the front.

Brooke was beaming. She was clearly happy, and the smile she gave Amy was triumphant. Amy smiled right back at her. She wasn't going to let anybody ruin the day.

'I *like* this,' Tasha declared.

Amy nodded. 'It's nice. Not exactly exciting . . .'

'I know,' Tasha said happily. 'That's why I like it.' She leaned over and stroked the water.

'Hold on to your paddle,' Amy warned.

'I will,' Tasha said dreamily. 'It's not like we really need them.'

'Not now, maybe,' Amy said. 'But if the water gets rougher, we'll need the paddles to steer the raft.'

'Mmm,' Tasha murmured. Her eyes were half-closed, and she looked very peaceful and contented. That was why Amy didn't mention what she thought she was hearing up ahead.

She could be wrong, of course. Her hearing was exceptional, but it wasn't always precise. That dim whooshing sound – it could just be the wind. But after a few seconds she knew the wind wasn't making that noise.

She tapped Dallas on the back. 'Dallas, are there rapids up ahead?'

Dallas was in the middle of telling Eric a story of how he'd gone on a white-water trip that nearly ended in disaster, and didn't seem to have heard her.

'Dallas,' she said again, this time more urgently.

'What?' he asked.

She repeated her question about the rapids.

'I don't see anything,' Dallas said. 'Relax! Didn't anyone ever tell you? – don't trouble trouble till trouble troubles you.'

How could she say that she was hearing something no one else could hear? Tentatively she touched Eric's shoulder and leaned forward so she could speak into his ear. 'Eric?' she whispered. 'I *hear* something.' Surely he could sense the urgency in her voice. He knew all about her skills; he had to pay attention to her.

But he was engrossed in Dallas's tale of disaster. She couldn't warn them of what was coming without revealing her special skills. And when the foaming water became visible, it was almost too late.

From the other raft came a cry that could barely be heard over the rumble of the water. 'There's a drop coming up,' Flora called frantically. 'It looks rough!'

Amy gripped her paddle as their raft nose-dived into the foam. The impact threw her backwards, and she heard Tasha shriek. There was water every-where, and as the raft careened through the huge waves, Tasha continued to shout. It was only when the water began to settle down that she realised why Tasha was still screaming. It wasn't just out of fear. Eric had gone overboard.

Amy jumped up and prepared to dive into the current, but Dallas grabbed her arm. She could have pulled free, but it wasn't necessary. Dallas had already thrown a rope to Eric, and Eric was holding on to it with both hands. The water was almost placid now, and Eric had no problem keeping his head above water as Dallas reeled him in. Eric was soaked when he climbed back into the raft, but he didn't appear to be at all disturbed by his accident. If anything, he looked a little cocky.

'Thanks, man,' he said to Dallas. 'I thought I could swim back, but there was a heavy undertow.'

'Are you okay?' Amy asked anxiously.

'Fine,' Eric said. 'It was no big deal.'

Amy was glad she hadn't jumped in after him. The way he'd been acting, he would probably have been offended by her attempt to rescue him.

'Is that going to happen again?' Tasha asked in a frightened voice. 'Will the river stay calm now?'

'Probably not,' Dallas told her. 'But don't worry, we've got plenty of rope! And if you can't get a grip on the rope, I'll save you.'

That seemed to calm Tasha a little, but her face was still tense. The water wasn't quite as calm any more. It seemed to be stirring, and more foam was appearing. The crashing noise of the turbulence increased. From the other raft, Flora yelled, 'Watch out for sleepers!'

Amy leaned forward and shouted into Dallas's ear, 'What's a sleeper?'

'A rock submerged below the surface,' he yelled back. She caught only a glimpse of his face, but he looked grim. Then she realised that they weren't even using their paddles. They didn't need them to move – the current was so strong it was swishing them downstream on its own.

The other raft had moved on ahead of theirs.

Through the shower of water that rose before them, Amy saw Flora turn and yell something. But now the water was barreling by with a thunderous, deafening roar, and even *she* couldn't make out Flora's warning. But she caught one word by lip-reading — it looked like *drop*. Now the raft was hurtling and crashing through the waves, and everyone in the raft was getting thrown about.

Amy's stomach lurched when she realised she couldn't see the other raft any more, but she didn't have long to consider the possibilities. Without any warning, their raft plunged downwards, in what seemed like a sheer drop. She was engulfed in water — it was in her eyes, her ears, her nose . . . with all her strength, Amy held on to Tasha and the raft and hoped that the guys in front could take care of themselves.

It was just as the raft began to level itself that she heard the screams from the other raft. 'Flora's overboard! She's underwater! She can't reach the rope!'

Andy was standing up in the raft, preparing to dive. 'Stay put!' Dallas barked at him, and dived off the raft himself. Amy watched as he pounded the swirling waters, moving in the direction of Flora's bobbing head. Then a massive surge of foam prevented her from seeing any more.

She and Eric began paddling furiously towards the riverbank, and the other raft followed them. For the zillionth time, Amy breathed a silent prayer of thanks for her exceptional strength – without it, she didn't think they'd be able to generate enough momentum to keep the boat from continuing downstream and to get them to the side. She couldn't imagine how the three normal kids in the other raft were going to make it.

But somehow they did, and the two rafts hit the bank almost simultaneously. Amy leaped out and dragged the raft onto the shore, with Eric and Tasha still occupying it. She hoped no one was watching. They'd have to wonder how a twelve-year-old girl was strong enough to pull so much weight.

Fortunately, Brooke and Willard were busy shouting at Andy. He was diving back into the raging water. Dallas and Flora were nowhere in sight.

Everyone collapsed on the bank, but there was no sense of relief – not until Dallas surfaced in the water with his arm across Flora's chest. Then Andy popped up. The two guys staggered out onto the bank. Dallas placed Flora on the ground and began performing artificial respiration.

In stunned silence, the others gathered around. Dallas had his mouth pressed against Flora's. He pounded on her chest in rhythmic motions. Then he breathed into her mouth again.

Amy had no idea how long this went on. But finally Dallas stopped working on her. Flora's limp body lay sprawled like a bruised rag doll. And even before Dallas spoke, they all knew the truth.

'She's dead.'

Memo to the Secretary: Transcript of Telephone Conversation with D

'Do you have anything to report?'

'All is proceeding as planned.'

'Good. Do they suspect?'

'No. There did appear to be an obstacle, but that obstacle has been eliminated.'

'What is your next step?'

'I plan to set up situations that will test skills.'

'Excellent.'

7

Brooke attempted to start a fire with some dry twigs. It was still very warm, but she was shivering. Amy couldn't blame her. The horror of what they had witnessed had chilled her to the bone too.

It was lunchtime, but no one was hungry. Andy stood alone, staring into space, lost in his own thoughts. Eric sat on a log, aimlessly picking the bark off a twig. Next to him, Tasha was huddled against a tree with her arms wrapped around her knees.

'I've been thinking about the Wilderness Adventure brochure,' she murmured. 'Remember how it said that no one had ever been seriously injured on an expedition?'

No one knew how to respond. 'I guess there's always a first time,' Eric said.

Brooke poked at the fire. 'I've never seen a dead person before.'

Amy had. She wished she could tell Brooke that having seen one dead person didn't make seeing another any easier.

She was still in a state of shock herself. She'd known there was always the possibility of accidents on this type of outing, but she'd never expected a tragedy of this magnitude. Her thoughts went back to the first moments after they realised Flora was gone.

The counsellors must have been well trained to handle emergencies and deal with a crisis, because Dallas didn't fall apart. He went right into action, ordering everyone to remain together at base camp. Then he lifted Flora's lifeless body in his arms and headed towards the trail that led back to the main road.

'I need someone to help me carry her,' he announced, after taking a few steps. He laid Flora's body down on the ground.

Andy stepped forward, but Dallas was looking directly at Willard.

'Why me?' Willard started to whine, but Brooke turned on him fiercely.

'Just do what he says,' she hissed. 'Can't you see how upset he is?'

Dallas was concealing his feelings well, though. To Amy he looked positively stoic. She figured he was putting up a good front so the others would remain calm. Inside, he had to be devastated. After all, despite their petty bickering, Flora was a lot more to him than simply a colleague.

Willard obeyed and shuffled over to the body. Between them, he and Dallas lifted Flora and took off on the trail. That had been almost two hours earlier, but the campers remained in a state of disbelief.

'I don't understand how it could have happened,' Tasha was saying, 'Flora was wearing a life jacket, just like the rest of us.'

'It was the undertow,' Eric said. 'It pulled her down.'

'Not right off,' Amy noted. 'Her head was above water.'

'I didn't notice that,' Brooke commented.

Amy shrugged. She didn't particularly feel like pointing out again how good her own eyesight was.

Then Andy spoke for the first time since the accident. 'I saw something too.'

His tone made them all turn to him expectantly. His eyes darted among them, as if he wasn't sure how they would react to what he wanted to say. But he said it anyway.

'Flora was floating above water until Dallas got to her. He pulled her down, and he hit her on the head with a rock.'

Amy stared at him, unable to speak. In fact, they were all speechless. Then Eric bluntly said what everyone was probably thinking. 'Are you nuts? Is this your idea of a joke?'

Andy wasn't offended. He didn't even blink. 'He killed her. Dallas killed Flora. I dived in the water too, remember. I saw him.'

'You're talking like a crazy person!' Tasha declared. 'Flora was his girlfriend! Why would he kill her?'

'I don't know,' Andy replied. 'Maybe they were fighting about something. Maybe he just didn't love her any more.'

Brooke was clearly dumbfounded. She was looking at Andy in utter perplexity, and Amy could see her predicament. She didn't want to contradict the boy she had a crush on, but at the same time, she was concerned about his sanity.

Tasha was aghast. 'Even if he didn't love her any more, he wouldn't kill her! Dallas isn't that kind of person!'

'How do you know that?' Andy asked her. 'We just met him the day before yesterday. None of us know what kind of a person he is.'

'You're sick,' Eric stated firmly. 'Dallas isn't a murderer.'

'I'm only telling you what I saw,' Andy replied calmly.

Eric was clearly angry. He took a step towards Andy, fists clenched. The expression on his face made Amy nervous, and she moved to place herself between the two boys.

'Andy just *thinks* he saw something,' she told Eric in a placating tone. 'You know what it's like underwater. Everything's distorted. That water is kind of muddy anyway, and there was a lot of foam.' Then she turned to Andy and spoke kindly. 'There was no way you could have seen anything. It's just not physically possible.'

He was gazing at her intently, and in his clear blue eyes she saw something she couldn't read. Was he hurt by her accusations? Did he think she was calling him a liar? She continued to speak gently. 'Andy, it was your imagination. That's not unusual. My imagination plays tricks on me all the time.'

Andy remained firm. 'I know what I saw.'

Tasha lost it. 'Stop it, stop it! Don't say that! How can you even *think* that? And don't you *dare* accuse Dallas. Do you realise how much pain he has to be in, how much he must be suffering?'

'I'm okay, Tasha.' Dallas emerged unexpectedly from the shadow of a tree. 'Calm down.' He walked over to her and put an arm around her shoulders.

'You don't know what he was saying,' Tasha wept.

Dallas's voice was soothing. 'It doesn't matter. We're all shocked and upset, and when people are feeling this way, they say things they don't really mean.'

He looked at Andy, who didn't look away.

'What happens now?' Brooke asked, breaking the tension.

'We carry on,' Dallas said simply.

Eric was taken aback. 'You mean this programme won't be cancelled?'

'No, that isn't how we do things at Wilderness Adventure,' Dallas told them. 'This is a survival programme, where we learn to deal with unexpected difficulties and obstacles. We don't give up, no matter what happens.'

Tasha had calmed down, and now she was looking at Dallas with unconcealed awe. 'But –

But how can you bear it?' she asked. 'You must be feeling awful!'

Dallas nodded and managed a sad smile. 'That's why I want us to carry on. I need to stay busy.'

Something occurred to Amy. 'Where is Willard?'

'He decided to bail out,' Dallas said. 'He was pretty shook up. He's not that strong, you know, physically or emotionally. He asked to leave the programme, and I didn't object.'

Amy was a little surprised. Willard hadn't been particularly enthusiastic about Wilderness Adventure, but he didn't seem any more freaked out than the rest of them by the accident. Still, he *was* kind of wimpy . . .

'Have you all eaten lunch yet?' Dallas asked them.

'No,' Tasha said. 'We weren't hungry.'

He nodded understandingly. 'But it's important for us to keep our strength up. You can't do much hiking or climbing on an empty stomach. You want to help me get lunch organised?'

Tasha was more than willing to do anything that would please Dallas. Within minutes, a picnic of salami, dried fruit, and nuts had been laid out on a blanket, and they all gathered around. Even Andy.

'Where did you take her?' Brooke asked.

'To the convenience store where we left the van,' Dallas told her. 'I called 911 and the Wilderness Adventure headquarters. An ambulance came for her.'

'What about the police?' Andy asked.

'Police?' Dallas said, as if he didn't know what the word meant.

Tasha's lips tightened. 'Why should the police come? It was an *accident*. Flora *drowned*.'

Amy looked at Andy anxiously, hoping he wasn't going to repeat his accusation. Dallas was trying so hard to deal with the situation and keep everyone calm. And she certainly didn't think it would help if Tasha got hysterical again.

'What about the bruise?' Andy asked.

Again Dallas was uncomprehending. 'What bruise?'

'The bruise on Flora's head,' Andy said.

Amy looked at him sharply. The others stared as if he was crazy.

'There was no bruise,' Dallas said. 'Did anyone see a bruise?'

Both Tasha and Eric shook their heads. 'I didn't see anything like that,' Brooke said. She edged closer to Andy. 'Why don't you go rest?' she suggested. 'It'll clear things up.'

Andy shook his head and rose suddenly. 'I'm going for a walk,' he announced.

'I'll go with you,' Brooke said, hopping up. 'Maybe talking will help.'

Andy was distracted but managed to give her an apologetic smile. 'No, thanks anyway, I'd rather be alone.' He turned away and strode off.

'Poor guy,' Brooke said. 'He's so confused and upset. I hate for him to be by himself.'

'We're all upset,' Dallas said.

'Yeah, but he's acting weird. I hope he doesn't do anything rash.'

'Maybe I should go after him,' Eric said uncomfortably, as if hoping someone would talk him out of it.

'No,' Amy said suddenly. '*I'll* go.' And before anyone could object, she got up and hurried off in the direction Andy had gone.

He had a head start on her, but even so, Amy was surprised not to see him in the distance. He was definitely a fast walker, or maybe he was running. No, she'd be able to hear pounding feet. She quickened her own steps, and, knowing that no one could see her now, moved at a pace that could win a marathon.

Finally she drew in close enough to hear his footsteps and was able to follow the sound. She found him sitting on a low rock by the stream where they washed every morning. He turned and watched her as she approached. His face revealed nothing, but at least he didn't seem angry that she'd come after him.

She sat down next to him on the rock. He didn't say anything, but she could tell he was waiting for her to explain why she was there. She did have a reason – but she was a little nervous about admitting it.

'I saw,' she began, and then amended her words. 'I *think* I saw a bruise on Flora's forehead.'

His eyebrows went up, but still, he didn't say anything.

'Maybe it was just my imagination,' she said quickly, even though by now she was sure it wasn't. 'It was very faint.' With intense focus, she could visualise it: a dull, purplish smudge under Flora's skin. She couldn't blame the others for not seeing it – *she* hadn't even noticed it at the time. It was only now, reflecting on the details of Flora's face, that she could see the almost imperceptible mark that hadn't even had time to become a real bruise.

She expected Andy to be pleased that someone

was confirming what he'd seen. But the expression on his face bore no resemblance to appreciation or gratitude. It was the oddest look he was giving her – a combination of suspicion, doubt, and something else. Fear? No, she had to be misreading him.

'Of course,' she said, 'Flora could have hit her head on a rock when she sank to the bottom of the river. It doesn't mean that Dallas intentionally struck her. Really, Andy, it's not possible that you saw him do that. You weren't that close to them when you dived in the water. Besides, the water was murky.'

'I *saw* him,' Andy said stubbornly.

What could she say? Nothing was going to change his mind, that much was clear. But she couldn't just walk away and leave him there alone. She didn't know why. Something seemed to hold her there, against her will.

No – not against her will. She *wanted* to stay with him. She knew it was more than the bond they'd recently established. It was something else, something she couldn't identify. And it made no sense at all. So she continued to sit there in silence. Complete silence. There was no breeze now, so even the leaves weren't rustling. The air was still and hot.

The noonday sun was just above them, and a trickle of sweat was coming down the side of her face. Even the birds seemed to have taken refuge from the heat – at least, she couldn't hear them. The silence was so thick she could hear her own heart beating. Or was it *his* heart?

She gazed at the stream. It looked inviting, with its promise of cool refreshment. She still had her bathing suit on under her shorts and T-shirt. She could take a dip right now . . .

Andy seemed to read her thoughts. 'I'm going for a swim,' he announced. He jumped off the rock and, with his back to Amy, pulled off his T-shirt. Then he ran to the stream and dived in.

Amy didn't follow him. She couldn't move. And she wasn't hot any more. A chill seemed to have formed deep inside her and was slowly spreading through her body. Was it possible? Had she really seen what was firmly planted in her mind? Or was *her* imagination playing tricks?

Andy rose from the water, and she knew this had nothing to do with a vivid imagination. On his back, on his right shoulder blade, was the mark of a crescent moon.

8

*I*mpossible, *impossible, impossible.* The word reverberated in her head. And yet, there was no mistaking what she had seen.

Amy lifted off her T-shirt, exposing the top of her two-piece bathing suit and something else, too. She slipped off the rock and started towards the stream. Her legs seemed to be walking on their own, without any effort, but she wasn't sure whether she was moving in fast-forward or slow-motion.

In the stream, she waded up to her waist. Andy stopped splashing around and stood there, waiting for her. When she reached him, she didn't speak. She just turned around so that he could see the mark on her back.

She expected to hear a gasp – some exclamation

of surprise or shock. When Andy said nothing, she turned back to face him. 'Andy?'

'I know,' he said simply. 'I could see it when we were rafting. You don't hide it, do you?'

'No,' Amy said. 'People think it's a birthmark, or a tattoo.'

'Yeah,' he said. 'Same here.' After a moment he added, 'But it's not a birthmark. Or a tattoo.'

'No,' Amy said again.

As if by unspoken agreement, they both moved out of the stream, onto the bank, and back to the rock where they'd been sitting. There was so much she wanted to ask, to say – but her tongue was tied. She couldn't organise the jumble of questions and thoughts that cluttered her mind, and she didn't know where to begin.

She didn't have to. Andy spoke first. 'I wondered, you know. When we met. The way you walked, what you could see and hear . . .'

Amy blanched. 'Wow. I really try not to draw attention to myself. Was it that obvious?'

'Only to another clone.'

There it was – that word. Now there were no secrets, and there was no turning back. 'So – you're like me.'

'Yes.' He gave her a crooked grin. 'No, actually, *you're* like *me*. I'm almost four years older than you. I came first.'

'But I thought Project Crescent only involved girls.'

'Apparently not,' he said. 'The project must have had several phases.'

Amy frowned. 'But my mother . . . she didn't tell me that.'

'Your mother?'

'She was a member of the project. She told me it was the first attempt to clone human lives.'

'Maybe that's what she was *told*,' Andy remarked. 'I don't think those scientists really knew what was going on.' He gazed at her with new interest. 'So your mother was a scientist on the project, huh? I guess you know a lot more about it than I do.'

'What *do* you know?' she asked him. 'And how did you find out?'

He didn't answer right away. She had a feeling this was the first time he'd ever talked about this to anyone, so it couldn't be easy. She remained quiet and let him take his time.

Finally he said, 'I think I always knew I was different. I mean, that there was something different about me. Even as a little kid I could do things other kids couldn't do. Is that how it was for you?'

'Not really,' she said. 'I never got sick when I was little, but that's the only thing that was different about me. I didn't start getting really strong until . . .' She hesitated. There was something about using the word *puberty* with a boy that made her embarrassed. 'Well, until recently,' she said lamely.

'My mother died when I was just a baby,' he went on. 'I knew I was adopted, my father told me when I was fairly young. But several years ago, he gave me a letter my mother had written before she died. She had told my father she wanted me to have it when I turned twelve.'

'What did it say?'

'Can't you guess?'

Amy shook her head.

'She wrote that I'd been part of a cloning experiment. That my genetic structure had been cloned from a combination of superior sources. She knew the director of the project, some doctor . . .'

'Dr Jaleski?'

'Yeah, that was the name. Anyway, he knew that my parents were looking for a baby to adopt, and he arranged for them to adopt me. She wanted me to know in case I ever wanted to search for my birth parents. I guess she didn't want me to waste my time.'

'Because you don't have birth parents,' Amy finished.

'Right.'

Amy thought this over. 'I guess, back then, Dr Jaleski didn't know what the project was *really* all about.'

'What do you mean?'

Amy realised Andy knew very little about them. So he told him all she knew – how the scientists of Project Crescent thought they were working towards the elimination of genetic disorders. How they discovered that the real purpose of their project was to create a master race of people, and that the people behind the project, the 'organisation,' had some disturbing goals.

'They sent the Amy babies away and destroyed the laboratory so the organisation would think the babies were dead.' She was about to go on and tell him that there seemed to be members of the organisation who knew the clones still existed, that they could be in danger – but she decided to wait and let him absorb this news first.

Because it was clearly news to him. 'You mean – there are more of me?'

'I guess so,' Amy said. 'If your experiment was like mine.'

'It must have been,' Andy said. 'We have the same mark.' After a moment his breath came out in a rush. 'Wow.'

Amy nodded. She remembered her own reaction when she first learned the truth about herself. But he couldn't be as stunned as she had been. At least he already knew he was a clone.

He spoke slowly. 'That doctor who was in charge . . .'

'Dr Jaleski?'

He nodded. 'I'd like to meet him.'

'You can't,' she said flatly. 'He's dead.' Her hand went to the hollow of her neck, where the crescent charm Dr Jaleski had given her usually dangled, and then she remembered she'd taken it off.

'Have you ever met any other Amys?' he asked her.

'Yes.'

'Where? How? What did it feel like?'

She couldn't blame him for having a million questions, but she didn't really feel like going into the history of her contact with Amys. None of the stories were that pleasant to remember. But she had to say something.

'It was . . . weird. We looked alike, but . . . we weren't I could feel a connection between us, though. Like we're sisters, I guess.'

He seemed satisfied. 'I felt it,' he said. 'Between us. The moment I met you, I felt a connection. Did you feel it?'

She thought back to the ride in the van, the conversation on the trail. She'd liked him, right off . . . yes, there was definitely *something*, she just couldn't put a name to it.

'But I don't feel like you're my brother,' she said out loud.

'No,' he said. 'It's not that kind of connection.'

Now another shiver was running through her . . . but this feeling was more of a tingle, an oddly thrilling sensation that she'd only experienced once before. And even though she knew her abilities did not include reading the future, she knew what was going to happen next.

They drew closer . . . they kissed.

It wasn't a long kiss, but it was enough for Amy to feel a wave of enormous guilt wash over her. What was she doing? This wasn't right. Desperately she tried to recall Eric's kisses, but she couldn't even conjure up his face. She leaned towards Andy, and they kissed again. Then she pulled away.

Her mind was reeling. What was happening to her? Was this simply the effect of one shock on top of another? Or were the emotions of a clone more exaggerated, more powerful than those of an ordinary human? If she could hear more, see more, then maybe she could *feel* more too.

He studied her face. 'I'm sorry. Maybe I shouldn't have done that.'

She couldn't agree. After all, he wasn't completely to blame.

'You're upset,' he said.

'I'm thinking about Eric.'

'Your boyfriend?'

She nodded, then buried her face in her hands. '*I* shouldn't have done that.'

Gently he pulled her hands away from her face. 'You couldn't help it,' he said.

She managed a half-smile. 'Why? Because you're so irresistible?'

'No. Because we're meant for each other.'

She gazed at him doubtfully. That sounded like a line from a corny love song.

'No, I mean it,' he said. 'Think about it, Amy. You

said the goal was to create a master race. Twelve Amys and twelve Andys . . . that's not a race.'

If her mind had been reeling before, now it was spinning out of control. Of *course*. Why hadn't she thought of this herself? 'Then, then that's what, what *this* . . .' She made a gesture indicating the two of them. 'That's what it's all about? We're – we're programmed to . . . to . . .' She tried to think of the right word.

'To mate,' he said.

She winced. That sounded so crude, like they were animals, exotic panda bears brought together in a zoo for the sole purpose of producing more panda bears. 'Well, maybe there's something genetic that makes us attracted to each other,' she said.

He brushed a lock of hair away from her face. 'Whatever's happening . . . it feels natural to me. Doesn't it feel natural to you?'

Amy looked at him searchingly. 'How can *we* even know what *natural* is supposed to feel like?'

'Like this,' he said softly. He moved closer and kissed her again. But then he pulled back.

She opened her eyes. He was looking over her shoulder, beyond her. She turned.

Brooke had just emerged from the bushes. Right

behind her was Eric. And it didn't take superhuman powers for Amy to know what they had seen. It was written all over their faces.

Brooke's face was pretty easy to read – it reflected pure anger. But Eric's face was something else. Anger, yes, but shock, pain, disbelief, that was all there too. He didn't give Amy long to read the expressions.

'Come on,' he said gruffly to Brooke. 'Doesn't look as if we're needed.' He tugged at her arm, and they both turned and disappeared into the bushes.

'Oh no,' Amy moaned. 'Oh no, oh no, oh no.' She got down from the rock. 'I have to go after him.'

'Wait,' Andy said, jumping down to her side. 'What are you going to tell him?'

'I don't know!' Hurt and shame churned in her stomach. 'I have to explain things. If he sees your mark—'

'What about my mark?'

'Eric knows what I am. If he knows that you're a clone too, he might understand.'

His eyes searched hers. 'But Amy . . . that's not fair to me. I don't want anyone to know what I am.'

He was right. It wouldn't be fair to Andy. But what else could she say to Eric, to make him understand? To make him forgive her? She had to think . . .

As she tried to concentrate, a dim spark of another thought hovered in the back of her mind. She attempted to push it aside, but it wouldn't go away. She let out a gasp.

Andy looked at her in alarm. 'What?'

'You *did* see Dallas hit Flora!'

'That's what I said.'

'Only I didn't believe you! No offence, Andy, it's just that I knew a normal person wouldn't be able to see what you said you saw. But *I* would have been able to see clearly underwater. Which means—'

Andy finished the sentence for her. 'I can too.'

'But *why*? Why would Dallas want to kill Flora? It doesn't make any sense.'

'Maybe she was in the way,' Andy said.

'In the way of what?'

He shrugged. 'I don't know. He could have some sort of plan.'

'A plan to do *what*?' Then she let out another gasp. 'Oh, Andy. You don't think – could it have something to do with us? Ohmigosh. Dallas could be from the organisation!'

He looked at her blankly. 'Huh?'

She remembered that she hadn't told him the whole story. 'The people who are looking for us,

Andy. You see, they haven't given up.' Quickly she related some of her own confrontations with the organisation.

He absorbed the information without freaking out, not even when she made it clear that he too could be in perpetual danger, just as she was.

'This whole thing could be a setup,' he said. 'Dallas might be working for *them*. He's new to Wilderness Adventure, remember? He could have joined up just to get close to us, you and me. Flora was in the way.'

'And so are the others!' Amy cried out. 'We have to warn them, Andy! Come on!'

He grabbed her hand. 'Wait,' he said. 'We don't want Dallas to know we suspect anything. Let me go back first, and get Eric alone. I'll show him my mark, and I'll tell him about myself. That way he'll have to believe me.'

She looked at him gratefully. She knew from experience how scary it was to give up the secret. 'Okay. I'll wait ten minutes.'

He took off, and Amy spent what seemed to be the longest ten minutes of her life before she too could start back to the campsite.

When she arrived, she didn't see Andy. But the

others – Brooke, Eric, and Tasha – were gathered around Dallas. They were all studying a map.

'We'll approach the mountain from this direction,' he was telling them. 'It's an easy climb. But we'll be coming down on this side, which is pretty steep, and that's when we'll use the ropes.'

Amy tried to catch someone's eye. When Tasha finally saw her, Amy beckoned. But Tasha's reaction made her heart sink. She just glared at Amy, then looked away. It was obvious that Eric and Brooke had told her what they'd seen. And even though Tasha might frequently be at odds with her brother, there was a family loyalty there. Tasha was not happy with her best friend.

Then everyone saw Amy.

'Hi,' Amy said, trying to sound natural. 'What's going on?'

Dallas smiled pleasantly. 'We've decided to do some abseiling this afternoon, Amy. Go get your hiking boots.'

'Okay,' Amy said, wondering where Andy was but not wanting to say his name aloud in front of Eric and the others. She walked across the campsite to her tent. Pushing the flap aside, she entered the dim interior.

It happened so fast, without any warning. Even her superior reflex skills couldn't prevent her from feeling the pain. A tiny shriek escaped her lips as something bit into her foot. Then her response-system clicked in, and with some real exertion, she pulled off the cold metal thing that gripped her. Stunned, she fell to the ground and rubbed her foot.

The tent flap opened, and Andy looked in. 'I heard you,' he said. 'What happened?'

Still shaky, Amy indicated the ugly metal contraption. 'What is it?'

He examined it. 'It's some kind of animal trap. Are you okay?'

She nodded, calmer now. 'If I wasn't so strong, and if my reactions weren't so quick, it would have broken my foot.'

'You wouldn't even have been able to pull it off,' Andy murmured. 'What was this thing doing in your tent?'

'It wasn't there before,' Amy said. 'Someone put it here.' She considered the contraption and shuddered.

Slowly Andy nodded. 'And I don't think it was meant to stop an animal.'

9

Once again Amy was aware of the unique physical connection she had with Andy. Simultaneously, their lips moved to form the name *Dallas*.

As if on cue, the counsellor's voice rang out. 'Amy! Andy! C'mon, you guys, let's get going!'

'Act like nothing happened,' Andy whispered, and started out of the tent. Amy followed close behind.

'Did you talk to Eric?' she asked softly. Andy wasn't listening and kept on walking. As they reached the others, it became clear that whether or not Andy had spoken to Eric, it wasn't going to make any difference. Eric wouldn't even look at her.

Tasha glanced at her through narrowed eyes, with lips still set in a tight line. She got a fierce, truly hostile look from Brooke. *That* came as no surprise. Brooke had 'claimed' Andy for herself their first day, and was no doubt thinking Amy had stolen her would-be boyfriend. Well, that was the least of Amy's problems.

Dallas was speaking. 'The ropes, the clips, and all the equipment have been divided evenly among your backpacks. The trail we'll be following is pretty wide, but there are a lot of twists and turns, with the path dividing several times. There's a potential for people to get lost, so I want everyone to stay together. Nobody goes on ahead of the group, okay?' His eyes went pointedly to Andy, and then to Amy. 'And if anyone finds that they can't keep up, give a yell and we'll slow down. I want to be able to keep my eye on everyone.'

He gave these instructions in a serious but friendly manner, as if this was the natural concern of any hiking leader. But Amy heard something else, another meaning in his comments. He didn't only want to protect them – he wanted to make sure no one got away from him.

Amy was determined to get Tasha or Eric alone

somehow. She had so much to explain, so much to tell them. But not now, that much was clear. As they started on the hike, Eric and Dallas walked side by side, with Andy a few feet behind them. That was good positioning, Amy thought. He'd be able to pick up on anything Dallas said.

Tasha was walking with Brooke, and Amy brought up the rear. She really didn't mind being alone. There was so much to think about. She had barely begun to deal with the impact of Flora's accident when she'd discovered that Amys weren't the only production of Project Crescent. To come face-to-face with a boy like Andy . . . and then the scare just now in her tent . . .

But it was Andy more than anything else that preoccupied her. Strange that she'd never considered the possibility of another set of clones. Had her mother really not known about a cloning experiment preceding hers? It wasn't as if she'd been exactly forthcoming about Amy herself.

And what about Dr Jaleski? Why hadn't he told Amy she had male counterparts? She thought back to the time they met. It was soon after she'd discovered the truth about herself. She'd already been aware of the doctor's existence, or at least his name – he'd signed her fake birth certificate and all the standard medical papers she'd needed for school. But as she began to deal with all the implications, the benefits, and the dangers of her life, her mother had decided it was time for them to meet.

He'd been so frank with her, saying he wanted her to be aware of all the facts, to know exactly who and what she was. He told her about the study, how the scientists had examined chromosomes and cellular structures in order to discover a means by which genetic disorders could be prevented from developing in a fertilised egg. He described how they had 'grown' the Amys in a controlled environment, how they had all been marked with a crescent moon for identification purposes, how they had been monitored and scrutinized. He'd explained how they had discovered the real motives of the government agency, the organisation that wanted to create this master race to take over the world.

As she relived the conversation in her mind, she remembered something else. She *had* asked Dr Jaleski if there were boy clones too! She even recalled how embarrassed she'd been to ask him the question. 'If they wanted to create a race, why did they just make girls? It takes a male and a female to, you know . . .'

And she could hear his answer. He had been pretty vague. He'd told her that the scientists themselves had wondered if maybe somewhere in the world a similar project was going on where male chromosomes were being cloned.

But according to Andy, Dr Jaleski had been the director of *his* project too. So at that time, when she and Dr Jaleski met, he had to know that the male clones existed. And he didn't tell her.

Why? Was he trying to protect her from something? Did he think she was too young to know that there was a boy out there somewhere, a boy who had been designed specifically for her to mate with?

She looked up ahead, where Andy was hiking, and wondered if it was as difficult for him as it was for her to walk this slowly. She could only see him from the back, and his T-shirt covered the mark. But she admired his broad shoulders, the golden streaks in his hair, his confident stride. What did the organisation have in mind for them? An arranged marriage? Maybe not with this Andy, though. It could be with another Andy . . .

She caught herself quickly. What was she *think-*

ing? Marriage! For crying out loud, she was twelve years old. Besides, she already had a boyfriend. At least, she *did* have a boyfriend.

And she wasn't giving up on that relationship.

Tasha and Brooke were talking now, and even though they were trying to keep their voices low, Amy could hear that they were talking about *her*.

'I am *not* sharing a tent with her any more,' Brooke was saying. 'Do you mind if I bunk with you for the rest of the week?'

'Sure,' Tasha replied. 'I don't really want to sleep alone. I can't believe Flora's gone.'

'I know. It's awful. I'm glad we're going on with the adventure, though.'

'Isn't Dallas incredible?' Tasha said. 'I don't know how he's coping. He must be so strong. Not just physically, emotionally too.'

'He's really something,' Brooke agreed.

Funny how both Tasha and Brooke thought Dallas's behaviour was so admirable. Amy thought it was strange. On the other hand, if Dallas had killed his girlfriend on purpose, it made perfect sense.

'Dallas is so cute,' Brooke continued. 'Too bad he's too old for us.'

'Yeah,' Tasha said wistfully. 'Too bad.'

'This is *not* turning out the way I thought it would,' Brooke grumbled. 'I figured, since Amy and Eric were already a couple, and Dallas and Flora were together, I would end up with Andy.'

'What about me?' Tasha asked indignantly.

'You could have been with Willard.'

'Gee, thanks,' Tasha retorted.

'It's strange about Willard, though, isn't it?' Brooke went on. 'Dropping out like that, without even saying goodbye?'

'I'm sure it happens often,' Tasha said. 'Especially after having to lug backpacks all the time. This thing's hurting my back.'

They were silent for a while, and then Brooke asked, 'Isn't Amy supposed to be your best friend?'

'Yeah. We've known each other forever. She lives right next door to me.'

'I guess she's not your best friend any more.'

Amy was grateful that Tasha didn't immediately affirm this. Brooke pressed her for a response.

'She just dumped your brother!'

'Yeah,' Tasha admitted. 'I'm pretty angry at her for doing that behind his back. I can tell he's really upset. But . . .'

'But what?'

'She's still my best friend,' Tasha said simply. 'We've had big fights before. I guess we'll probably get over this.'

Amy's heart was singing. Tasha had to realise that Amy could hear everything she was saying. So now she knew that Tasha would speak to her again, eventually. And that was important – because her first priority was to let the others know that Andy had been telling the truth. Dallas *had* killed Flora. Tasha would be her link to reaching Brooke and Eric, to let them know they had to get away from Dallas and whatever diabolical plans he had.

At least Dallas had been telling them the truth when he said that the hike up the mountain would be easy. The incline was so slight that it took a while before Amy realised they had even started up the mountain. She wasn't having to exert herself any more than when they were walking on flat ground.

Tasha wasn't having as easy a time of it, though. Amy could hear her panting, and she knew Tasha was really feeling the extra weight of the pack. After just a few more moments, Tasha stopped walking.

'I can't carry this thing,' Amy heard her telling Brooke. 'It's too heavy!' There was panic in her voice. Amy started walking faster, to catch up with them and offer to take on Tasha's burden.

But Brooke had already called Dallas, who had retraced his steps to hear Tasha's complaint. He didn't scold her and seemed understanding of her problem. He waved for the others to gather around him.

'Tasha's the smallest one here, and she's having a hard time balancing her backpack with the extra equipment,' he announced. 'But we need the equipment she's carrying for the abseiling. Who can propose a solution to this problem?'

'My pack isn't too heavy,' Eric said. 'And there's space in it. I can take some of Tasha's load.'

'Yeah, me too,' Andy said quickly.

Dallas beamed. 'Excellent! This is exactly the kind of response I was hoping to get. One of the goals of Wilderness Adventure is to help out members of the team who aren't as strong as the others.'

Tasha didn't look too happy about that. 'But it's not fair for anyone to carry more than their share.'

Dallas put a fatherly arm around her shoulder. 'It's okay,' he said soothingly. 'It's not your fault that you're shorter than everyone else here! And you make up for your lack of height with your sparkling personality.'

To Amy's dismay, Tasha fell for the feeble compliment. She gazed up at Dallas in utter devotion and gratitude. Dallas took the pack off her shoulders, opened it, and distributed most of the contents among Andy, Eric, and himself.

'I can take some of her stuff,' Amy offered.

Dallas shook his head. 'You're not much taller than Tasha, Amy. I think the boys and I can handle this.' But his eyes lingered on her – just long enough to make her think that he knew perfectly well she could handle a lot more than she was carrying now.

She looked at Andy, and he gave an almost imperceptible nod, indicating that he was thinking the same. But then she realised that Eric had intercepted the look. His eyes darkened, and he turned away.

It hurt – but she'd have to deal with that later. The most important mission right now was to convince the others that Dallas posed a threat. Once they believed that, she would do everything possible to make amends with Eric.

They moved on up the mountain. 'This isn't much of a climb,' Eric commented. 'I'm not even breaking a sweat.'

'Abseiling isn't mountain climbing,' Dallas told them. 'Getting up the mountain isn't the goal. It's the coming down that matters.'

Amy didn't see how coming down this mountain could be any more difficult than going up it. At least, not until they reached the top. Then she realised they were now on a cliff.

The group greeted the sight in silence. Tasha spoke first, and her voice trembled. 'We're supposed to climb down *that*? We'll fall off!'

Amy couldn't blame her for sounding petrified. From this side, it was a sheer drop from the top of the mountain to the ground. A *long* drop.

'How high are we?' she asked.

'About two hundred feet,' Dallas replied. 'This is considered a beginner's mountain for abseiling. Like a nursery slope for skiers.'

'Not like any nursery slope I ever saw,' Brooke commented. 'Are you sure this is for beginners?'

'Brooke, I'm a certified counsellor,' Dallas said patiently. 'Now, gather round and let me show you how we do this.'

The climbing ropes were arranged over a bulging section of the cliff, and Dallas demonstrated how their use of the ropes and the mechanical devices would control their speed as they made their way down the steep slope. He described the exhilaration they'd feel when they stepped off the top, and the sense of accomplishment when they reached the bottom.

'If we're in one piece,' Tasha murmured.

Dallas smiled. 'I won't let anything happen to you, Tasha.'

Great, Amy thought. And what about the rest of us? Normally, she wasn't nervous about doing anything physical. But with a two hundred-foot drop to the hard ground, even a physically superior clone could be injured. She couldn't help thinking that this might be part of Dallas's scheme to – to do what? If he was from the organisation, he wouldn't want either her or Andy to be hurt.

But he'd killed Flora just to get her out of the way. Who knew what he had in mind for Eric, Tasha, and Brooke?

So when Dallas asked, 'Who would like to go first?' Amy spoke up quickly.

'I will.' She could almost see her mother's reproving look. But this wasn't showing off. She wanted to check out the ropes before anyone with a weaker body and slower reactions took a turn.

Once she was hooked up and in position, the ropes clipped onto her belt felt strong and secure. She inched her way backwards over the edge.

It was a strange sensation. There were plenty of jutting rocks to grab on to, and she knew that even if her grip slipped, the ropes would keep her from plummeting to the ground. Even so, she swallowed repeatedly as she eased herself down the vertical drop. It was definitely unnerving. And she couldn't see what was going on above her on the cliff. What if Dallas suddenly pulled out a sharp knife and cut the rope? She hoped Andy was watching him carefully.

When her feet touched solid ground, she wasn't sure if what she was feeling was one of accomplishment or just plain old relief. She undid her clips and let the ropes go. Gazing back up at the group on top of the cliff, she saw that Eric was coming down next. Finally, she'd have him alone for a few minutes – assuming he made it to the bottom . . .

Watching him carefully, she was unsure of what she would do if the rope broke. Rush to catch him? But the rocks he'd hit as he fell could destroy him before he reached the bottom. Could she somehow climb the mountain rapidly to rescue him? Maybe –

but if Eric wasn't already dead, he'd probably kill her for making him look less manly in front of the others.

Fortunately, she wasn't called upon to do anything at all. Eric handled the climb well and reached the ground safely.

She rushed towards him as he unclipped his ropes. 'Eric, you have to listen to me,' she began.

'No, I don't,' he replied. 'Amy, I saw what I saw. There's nothing you can say that will change that.'

She clutched his arm tightly to keep him from walking away. 'Eric, Andy isn't a regular person. He's like me.'

Eric blinked. 'You're saying he's a clone?'

Amy nodded. 'There was another Project Crescent before mine. They made boys first. Then they made the girls. And we're designed to go together, so that we can—'

'I think I can guess the rest,' Eric said. 'I can't believe this is your excuse for making out with that guy. What's the deal here – you two are programmed so you can't resist each other? Like – like it's your destiny to be together or something?'

'I think it is something like that,' Amy admitted. 'Look, this doesn't mean Andy and I have to get married. But we're going to have some kind of relationship. This doesn't have to affect you and me, Eric. I want us to stay together, and . . .' Her voice began to falter. She'd never seen his eyes so cold.

'It's not just that,' she said rapidly. 'We could be in danger, all of us. Did you hear what I said? Andy's a clone, like me, and that means he really saw what he said he saw under the water. Dallas killed Flora, Eric. I don't know what it's all about, but we have to get out of here, away from him.'

Eric wasn't even looking at her now. His eyes were on the mountain. 'Either he's lying to you or you're lying to me. Your new boyfriend doesn't look like much of a clone from here.'

Amy turned, and caught her breath. Midway down, Andy was dangling from the rope, and he wasn't within reach of anything on the mountain to grab on to.

'You see!' she cried out to Eric. 'It's Dallas, he let the rope out too fast! He wants Andy to fall!'

'So what are you worried about?' Eric said. 'If he's a clone, he'll just stub his toe, right?'

'Don't be an idiot!' Amy shouted. She ran towards the mountain, not knowing what she was going to do but sure that she could do something.

Even if it meant revealing the special nature she and Andy shared . . .

But she didn't need to do anything extraordinary. Andy had managed to swing in closer to the mountain, and now he was holding on to a protruding rock. Amy released her breath as he made his way safely to the bottom. She rushed over to him.

'Are you okay?'

Andy nodded. 'Did you see that?' he asked. 'I know Dallas was trying to make me fall. Amy, we have to get out of here. *Now*.'

'But we can't leave the others,' Amy declared. 'They have to come with us.'

Andy sighed. 'Good luck trying to talk them into it. They won't come along, Amy.'

She looked at Eric, saw the cold anger radiating from his eyes, and knew Andy was right. Eric wasn't about to trust them. Nor would Brooke, she was certain of that.

As for Tasha . . . Amy looked up. Her best friend was abseiling now. She was coming down inch by inch, fortified by the words of encouragement Dallas was calling to her. Tasha wouldn't listen to anything they might say against Dallas. Dallas had become her own personal idol.

Andy was right. She and he weren't exactly the most popular people in the group. No one would believe anything they had to say. But how could she leave her best friend, when she might be in serious danger? And Eric . . . would he ever forgive her? Would he ever understand?

'Come on,' Andy urged, 'we have to go before Dallas gets down. He'll think we've just gone back to the campsite, and that will buy us some time before he starts searching.'

Amy thought quickly. 'Okay. We'll go get help and then come back for the others.'

'Exactly,' Andy said. He took her hand. Together they began to walk away.

Amy didn't turn around to say goodbye to Eric. She didn't dare. Because even the strongest girl in the world couldn't hold back tears.

10

They walked quickly, but not until they were out of Dallas's line of vision did they pick up speed.

'We'll head towards the main road,' Andy said. 'Then we'll find the convenience store where we left the Winnebago. We can call for help from there.'

Amy envisioned her mother's reaction when she got the phone call. It hadn't been easy for Amy to talk Nancy into letting her go on this trip, and now, once again, her mother's fears were coming true. Amy'd be lucky if her mother ever let her out of her sight again.

They were in an area now that Amy didn't recognise. The terrain didn't look at all familiar.

'We should find the trail we took from the main road,' she said.

'No, that won't work. It would be too easy for Dallas to come after us.'

'He's just one guy, Andy, and he's not all that big. The two of us together could take him on.'

'The two of us together can't stop a bullet,' he replied grimly.

'He's got a *gun?*'

Andy nodded. 'I saw it in his pack the first day. I even asked him about it. He said he always carried a gun on these expeditions, for protection, just in case he ran into any wild animals.'

'What kind of wild animals?' Amy asked uneasily.

'Probably the same kind that the trap in your tent was meant for.'

'Us,' she whispered.

'Yeah.'

He took her hand, and she didn't object. She even let him lead, which was an unusual experience for her.

'Are you sure we're going in the right direction?'

'I'm sure,' he said.

'Are you really? We don't have a compass or a

map or anything. How can you tell this is the way to the road?'

Andy wasn't annoyed by her doubts. He even grinned. 'Listen.'

She concentrated on sounds. But with the exception of their footsteps and the rustling as they pushed aside bushes, she heard nothing unusual. 'What are you hearing?'

'Traffic,' he said. 'Cars, trucks, something. It's pretty far away, but it gets louder as we continue in this direction.'

She looked at him admiringly. 'Wow. Your ears are better than mine.'

'I'm sure you do some things better than me,' he said comfortingly. 'How fast can you run?'

'I'm not sure,' she admitted. 'I never timed myself. I'm fast, I know that. And my eyesight is amazing. I can see three times farther than a regular person.' It dawned on her that she'd never felt so free talking about herself before. Even with friends like Tasha and Eric, who knew what she was, she couldn't speak as frankly. She always thought it sounded like she was bragging.

But Andy understood. 'That's definitely farther than I can see,' he told her.

'I guess it makes sense that we wouldn't be exactly identical,' Amy said. 'After all, you're several years older than I am.'

'And a different sex,' Andy added. 'I mean, our bodies are different.'

'No kidding,' Amy said without thinking, and then she blushed.

'Sorry, I didn't mean to embarrass you.' He stopped walking, and his hand on hers tightened.

'What?' Amy asked.

'Shhh. Listen. I hear something behind us.'

This time Amy's ears heard it too. But she couldn't identify the noise. Her voice dropped to a whisper. 'It doesn't sound like footsteps.'

'No,' Andy said softly. 'Not *human* footsteps.'

'An animal? Maybe it's just a rabbit.'

'No, it's bigger than a rabbit.'

She looked at him. 'Then why are we just standing here? We should run!'

'We might be better off climbing a tree. If it's a wolf or a panther we can't outrun it.'

'Okay, but let's do *something*!'

Only it was too late to do anything at all. Something huge and black was lumbering towards them.

Amy was barely able to register that it was a bear before it lunged at her.

Huge, furry arms enveloped her body. She struggled to free herself, but the animal's strength was beyond anything she had ever encountered before. With her face pressed against the bear's chest, she couldn't breathe.

Then she felt something else – a force, pushing from behind the bear. With a loud grunt, the bear released her and turned towards Andy. He was in a pose she dimly recognised from a poster in Eric's bedroom. As the bear got closer, he went into action. His leg went up amazingly high, and he kicked the bear in the chest. The bear staggered backwards. Andy didn't stop. He continued kicking, aiming the blows at the animal's chest. The bear seemed stunned. Andy grabbed Amy's hand and they ran.

She couldn't tell how long they'd been running, but when they finally stopped to rest, she felt pretty sure the bear wasn't too close behind. They collapsed on the ground, still holding hands. They'd been running so hard and fast, she was actually out of breath, and Andy was too.

'You were incredible!' she told him when she could speak. 'What were you doing?'

'Kick boxing,' Andy told her breathlessly. 'I take lessons. Karate, judo, kung fu, tai chi, all that stuff.'

'Wow,' Amy breathed. 'For exercise?'

'And self-defence,' he said. 'San Francisco's a big city. Not as violent as some, but it's good to be prepared.'

'But why do you need martial arts for self-defence?' she asked him.

'It worked on the bear, didn't it?'

'Sure, but it's not like you run into grizzlies on San Francisco's streets. We're stronger than humans. You could just punch out anyone who attacked you.'

'Yeah, I know. But I'd rather use real fighting skills, the kind any person can develop. It makes me feel more normal.'

She smiled at him. Her mother would approve of that. Not to mention the fact that he'd just saved Amy's life.

Amy approved too. She liked the fact that he possessed the extraordinary skills she did but didn't rely on them. She liked everything about him.

They allowed themselves only a few moments to rest. 'We need to get out of the woods and onto the road before dark,' he said. 'I know we've both got good night vision, but I don't particularly want to test it in the woods.'

She agreed. 'Which way?'

He cocked his head thoughtfully and listened. Then he pointed. 'This way.'

Amazing, she thought for the zillionth time that day. She still couldn't hear any traffic. But after walking for a while, she *did* hear something interesting.

'Frogs,' she said.

'Huh?'

'I hear frogs. That means we must be close to water.'

He frowned. 'It must be an extension of the river. I hope it's not rapids. We may have to swim across.'

'I don't hear any rushing water,' Amy told him. 'It shouldn't be a problem.'

She was partly right. The water they encountered was still. But it was also about a hundred feet below them. And there were no abseiling ropes to get them down the steep embankment.

She estimated that the distance to the river was about fifty feet. Luckily, a bridge spanned the gap. They made their way alongside the cliff towards it.

'Have you ever walked on a rope bridge before?' Andy asked her.

'No.'

'I have. It's a weird sensation, because it doesn't feel very sturdy. But don't worry, they're stronger than they look.'

She certainly hoped so. The bridge that dangled between two trees on opposite sides of the crevice didn't exactly inspire confidence. At least they wouldn't be on it very long.

The bridge was narrow, and they would have to walk single file. 'Do you want me to go first and test it?' Andy asked.

'Do you think it's strong enough to support the two of us together?' she asked. The water below didn't look deep enough to drown in, but there were plenty of huge rocks jutting out.

He grabbed a rope and shook it. The bridge swung, but it remained firm. 'Yeah, it's okay.'

Tentatively, gripping the ropes on both sides, Amy stepped onto the swaying bridge. She felt Andy step on behind her. 'You okay?' he asked.

'So far,' she said nervously.

'Just keep looking straight ahead, and don't look back,' he instructed her. 'It could make you dizzy.'

She had absolutely no intention of looking back,

or down, or anywhere except the end of the bridge, where she could step onto firm land.

'I wonder how long this bridge has been here,' he mused. 'Hundreds of years, maybe.'

Amy moaned. 'Andy, that doesn't make me feel better.'

'Well, I'm just saying, if it's lasted this long . . .'

'Andy!'

'Okay, okay, I won't say another word.' He laughed.

The laugh did make her feel better, and she hoped he didn't think she was being a wimp. Walking on such an unsteady surface was giving her stomach butterflies, but once they were almost halfway across the bridge, she started to relax. Then it happened. The bridge started to sway.

'Andy? What are you doing?' Amy shouted as she gripped the ropes more tightly.

'I'm not doing anything. It must be a gust of wind.'

'There isn't any wind,' she shouted again. Then the whole bridge seemed to ripple. 'Andy, what's happening?'

'I don't know,' he said.

Ahead of her, the bridge looked fine. Gathering

her courage, she turned her head, but Andy's broad shoulders blocked her view of the other end, and the movement made her dizzy. Another ripple, this one stronger, made her gasp.

'Andy! Is there something happening behind you?'

He turned. 'I can't see, the sun's in my eyes. Wait, there's something in the tree back there!'

'What is it?'

'I don't know!'

The bridge wasn't just swaying from a mere ripple any more. Now it was positively shaking. An ominous chopping sound reached her ears, and Andy let out a shout.

He pulled her around and circled her arms around his waist. 'Amy, hold on to me!'

And the next thing she knew, they were falling.

11

Holding on to Andy as tightly as possible, all Amy could think was that they'd crash on the rocks together, their blood and guts spilling into the river, joined together forever . . . Strange, how calm she felt. Because there was nothing that could be done now, as they sailed down into eternity . . .

She wanted one last glimpse of his face and stretched her head back to look up. And saw a remarkable sight.

Andy's arms were above his head, clinging to a heavy rope. And suddenly they weren't falling to their deaths any more. They were high-wire per-formers, acrobats in a show. They were *alive*. Alive, intact, and dangling from a rope just a few feet above the edge of the river.

She let go of him and dropped into the shallow river. He followed her. They waded through the water, staggering up to shore, where they collapsed in a heap. There, on the damp, muddy bank, they clung to each other silently.

Tears began to stream down Amy's face. Of all the close encounters in her life so far, of all the scary moments when she'd thought she was in serious trouble, this had been the worst.

She was so accustomed to being the strong one, the smart one, the one who saved other people. It felt good to be held by someone as strong as – if not stronger than – she was. Another new sensation. A whole new kind of relationship. She didn't think she had ever felt so completely safe, so completely trusting of anyone.

'What happened?' she asked.

'The ropes broke.'

'They broke? Or were they cut?'

'I don't know. I thought I saw someone in the tree where the ropes were anchored.'

'Dallas?'

'Maybe. Or it could have been an animal, chewing on the rope. We were lucky, Amy. I just grabbed on to the rope and hoped it was short enough to keep us from hitting the ground.'

'Like bungee jumping,' she murmured. A sport she'd never been interested in trying.

'Yeah. Funny, I never wanted to do that.'

They really were so much alike.

'We can't stay here,' he said. 'If Dallas cut the rope, he must have figured out that he didn't kill us.'

Amy got to her feet. 'You know, I think I hear that traffic now.' Then she realised that was just wishful thinking. She heard nothing at all.

But Andy nodded. 'We're not too far.' He moved confidently, leading her through some prickly bushes and over a large rock. 'Look! There's the trail.'

And so it was – the same trail they'd hiked on just two days before. Amy recognised a rock formation and a tree with limbs so low they'd had to climb over them.

She had a good memory for directions. If she went somewhere once, she could find her way back easily. But she didn't think she could have found this trail on her own.

'You're incredible,' she told him.

He didn't deny it. 'We're both incredible,' he said. 'That's why we're so good together.'

A deliciously warm shiver went through her. The Project Crescent scientists must have known what they were doing. She'd never felt so attached, so connected. So *not* alone.

For one fleeting moment, Eric's face appeared in her mind's eye, but she refused to feel guilty. There was nothing she could do about this. What was happening between her and Andy – it was meant to be.

They walked hand in hand, in quiet contentment. Every now and then, Amy heard a car or truck, and each time it was a little louder. It wasn't much longer before they emerged from the wooded area and arrived at the two-lane highway. The sun had started to set, but not too far down the road, she saw the back of the convenience store.

In unspoken agreement, they broke into a run. The Winnebago was still in the parking area where they'd left it. Was it really only a couple of days ago that they'd climbed out of it, so full of excitement and anticipation?

But when they reached the entrance of the store, they stopped short.

The interior was dark, and there was a sign on the door: CLOSED FOR VACATION. The dates that followed this announcement indicated that the store wouldn't reopen for two weeks.

They both stared at the sign in dismay. 'Oh, great,' Andy groaned. 'Now what are we going to do?'

Amy didn't answer. She was still staring at the sign. 'Andy, what's today's date?'

'The fourteenth.'

'This store closed for vacation yesterday,' she said.

'Yeah, so what?'

'Dallas said he and Willard brought Flora here. This is where they called for an ambulance. That was this morning, and the store was already closed.'

Andy considered this. 'Maybe there's pay telephone around the side of the store.'

There was — but it was broken. And from the layer of dust on it, Amy could tell it had been broken a long time.

She gazed down the empty highway. 'How far are we from a town?'

'Not a clue,' Andy said. 'I remember we stopped for gas somewhere.'

'Yeah, and then we were on the road for another hour before we got here,' Amy said. 'I don't remember seeing anything. So I suggest we start walking in the other direction. Maybe there's a gas station or something closer.'

'Okay,' Andy agreed. 'But why walk when we can ride?'

'You mean take the Winnebago?'

He shook his head. 'I'm sure it's locked, and even if we could break in, I don't know a thing about hotwiring a car.'

She smiled. 'I'm glad to hear you're not an experienced car thief. So how are we going to ride?'

'We'll hitchhike.'

Amy hesitated. That was something she'd sworn to her mother that she would never do. The newspapers were full of horror stories about young people who willingly got into cars with drivers who weren't picking them up out of the kindness of their hearts.

But after what they'd been through today, nothing could be more dangerous. Besides, she wasn't alone. She was with Andy. And their combined strength and energy could overpower pretty much anyone.

'Okay,' she said, and they walked towards the highway.

She was ready to make a fist with her thumb stuck out in the traditional manner, but there wasn't car in sight. And she couldn't hear anything coming.

When a car did finally come along, they both stuck out their thumbs eagerly. The car didn't stop or slow down. A few minutes later another car appeared, but this driver wasn't any more willing to pick them up than the first one.

It dawned on Amy that neither of them looked like the kind of hitchhikers anyone would want to pick up. They were both dirty, wet, and bedraggled.

'I think we'd better start walking,' she said.

'Wait a minute,' Andy said. 'Something's coming.'

It was a black sedan, and it wasn't going very fast. 'I think it's slowing down,' Amy said excitedly. She stuck out her thumb and smiled brightly.

Sure enough, the car edged over to the side of the road and cruised to a stop just in front of them. Amy ran over to the open window on the passenger side. Andy was right behind her.

'Sir, could you give us a lift—?' she began, and then the shock of recognition hit her.

'Mr Devon!'

'Get in the car,' he said.

She felt Andy's hand on her shoulder, and she turned. Andy was looking at the driver too, but there was no mistaking the horror and fear on his face.

'Run!' he yelled. 'Amy, run!'

Memo to the Secretary: Transcript of Telephone Conversation with D

'What is the current situation?'

'The escape has taken place.'

'Is there a problem?'

'Not at all. Everything is under control.'

'Where is the subject now?'

'Highway 61. Under observation.'

12

It must have been her instinctive trust of Andy, her sense of connection to him, that made her obey him so immediately. She could still hear Mr Devon calling, 'Amy, Amy, come back!' The sound of his voice followed her as she and Andy ran into the woods. They kept on running until she couldn't hear the shouts any longer. Then Andy stopped.

'Stay here,' he ordered her. He jumped and grabbed the limb of a tree with both hands. Hoisting himself up, he climbed higher. Amy had no idea what he was doing.

'I can't see him,' he said climbing back down. 'I don't think he's following us.'

'I could have told you that,' Amy said. 'I would

have heard him.' After a second, she added, 'So would you.'

'Yeah, well, I wanted to make sure.' Andy was still breathing heavily. He sank down on the ground and leaned against the trunk of the tree.

'Do you smoke?' Amy asked him suddenly.

'No, why?'

'I was just wondering, because you're so out of breath.'

'You can't blame me,' Andy said. 'That was a shock! And I don't mind telling you, I was seriously scared.'

Amy sat down next to him. 'Why?'

He was obviously surprised. '*Why*? You saw who that was. You recognised him.'

She nodded. 'Mr Devon.'

He uttered a harsh laugh. 'Mr Devil, you mean.'

'*What?*'

He gazed at her steadily. 'I guess you didn't have the same experience with him that I did.'

She considered this. 'He and I have had some pretty weird encounters,' she acknowledged. 'But I always thought he was on my side.' She amended that. '*Our* side.'

'Yeah, I'm sure that's what he'd like you to think,' Andy said bitterly.

'How do *you* know him, Andy?'

He didn't answer and looked away.

'It must have been something very bad,' she said gently. 'I was surprised when I saw him. But *you* completely freaked out.'

He still wouldn't look at her, but at least he spoke. 'It isn't easy looking into the face of the man who kidnapped you.'

'Mr Devon kidnapped you?'

Finally he faced her. 'I was just a little kid, four years old. He showed up at my nursery school, and I guess he convinced the teacher he was a friend of my dad's. Anyway, he took me away . . .' His voice faltered.

'Away where?' she prompted him.

'I don't know. But I remember, everything was white. It must have been a hospital. There were people looking at me. And needles.' He shuddered. 'It's all kind of hazy now. Almost like a dream. But it wasn't a dream, Amy. It was real. And I'll never forget that face. You can't imagine how many times since then I thought I saw him again.' After a moment he added, 'Maybe I did.'

'I thought I saw him in a hospital once,' Amy said slowly. Her mind called up the unpleasant image

. . . a hospital in New York, all those other Amys, the evil Dr Markowitz, who was in charge of the experiments. Mr Devon appearing in the doctor's office . . . for a moment, she had thought he was with the organisation too. But when she jumped from the hospital window, he was there to save her – or was he? It was all so confusing and hazy now, just the way Andy described *his* experience. Only she couldn't be as sure as he was that it was *not* a dream.

'He's a bad man, Amy. And it's all starting to make sense to me now. He must be one of those people who wants to create a new race. He's been following us, watching us. Or maybe he had spies who reported on us. Dallas could have been one of them!'

Amy struggled to absorb all this. Something kept bothering her, though. 'But he's helped me,' she told Andy. 'He keeps popping up when things get weird, and every time he does, I learn something more. He's given me information and warned me away when I was close to trouble. He saved my life once.'

'In other words, he's always there,' Andy said. 'Which means he's watching you, too.'

She put a hand to her head. It was starting to ache from all the confusion. From something else too. Her stomach let out an audible grumble, and Andy didn't have to be a clone to hear it.

'You're hungry,' he said. 'So am I.'

'What are we going to do?' she wondered out loud. It was dark now. 'We could hunt for berries and nuts, I guess. Mushrooms . . .'

'They can be poisonous. Do you know how to identify the edible ones?'

'No,' she admitted.

'It doesn't matter,' he said. 'We wouldn't be able to find them in the dark anyway.'

She eyed him curiously. 'Really? Don't you have good night vision?'

'Not *that* good.'

She looked around. *She* didn't have any problem seeing in the dark.

Andy stood up. 'We have to get some food.'

'From where?'

'The convenience store. You stay here, I can find my way back to it.'

Amy gaped. 'You're going to break into the store?'

'Amy, you want food, don't you? Once we're

out of this mess, I'll pay the store owner for the damages. Look, there isn't any alternative.'

'No, I guess not,' she murmured.

He took off in the direction of the road. She sat back against the tree trunk and tried to unravel the mess in her mind.

Why was she so bothered by Andy's attitude towards Mr Devon? She had certainly had doubts about the man. He was mysterious, that was for sure. But she recalled the fear she'd seen in Andy's eyes . . . *she'd* never been afraid of Mr Devon. On the other hand, she didn't really know Mr Devon.

You don't really know Andy, either.

She responded to the little voice in the back of her head. It's different with Andy. It's like we're related. We come from the same place, we both have the mark.

But that didn't silence the little voice. *Anyone can get a tattoo in the shape of a crescent moon.*

She was vaguely aware of a slight increase in her heart rate. What proof did she really have that Andy was a clone? What had he actually done that was so out of the ordinary? He walked fast . . . but so what? Lots of people did. He'd said he heard the road traffic from deep in the woods, but there was so little traffic to be heard. And he'd used martial arts to fight the bear, not regular physical strength. Maybe he didn't *have* the physical strength. Maybe he studied martial arts not as a way to seem more normal, but because he *was* normal.

Amy's head spun with each creeping doubt.

And what about Flora? Amy reminded herself that only someone with extraordinary vision could have seen her under the murky water.

He *said* he saw Dallas kill Flora. How do you know he was telling the truth?

And the connection she felt with Andy – was it all in her mind?

And if he wasn't like she was . . . who was he? Was he one of *them?*

She thought back, mentally reliving every minute since meeting him, going over every conversation, searching for clues . . .

When she heard his footsteps approaching, she still hadn't come to any real conclusion. She cautioned herself not to let her doubts show. She couldn't let Andy know what she was thinking. She was alone in the woods with him, and she had no idea what to expect from him any more.

He dropped a big sack onto the ground. 'Ready for a junk-food feast?' he asked. He pulled out bags of crisps, candy bars, and sodas. Amy tried to look pleased with the pile of goodies. She realised that she'd completely lost her appetite.

'Did you have trouble getting into the store?' she asked him.

'Not really,' he said. 'I broke down the back door.'

She spoke carefully. 'I guess that's the first time you've ever done anything like that.'

He grinned. 'Once, I forgot the combination to my school locker, and broke in to get a book I absolutely needed for class. You should have seen the custodian when he discovered the damage. He thought a bomb had exploded.'

His smile was contagious, and she found herself responding. It was impossible to think she might really be in danger. Still . . . if only there was some sort of way she could test him . . .

'What was that?' she asked suddenly.

'What?'

'I just heard something.'

His brow furrowed. 'Yeah, I hear something too.'

'Look!' she cried out, and pointed. 'Oh, it's gone!'

He looked in the direction she'd indicated. 'It was just a deer,' he said. 'Nothing to worry about.'

Nothing to worry about. Not from any deer, at least. Because she hadn't heard or seen anything. And if Andy said he had, he was lying.

She tried to eat a little, all the while thinking, planning. She half-listened to Andy as he pondered aloud what Dallas must have done with Flora's body and what had happened to Willard. Then she produced a yawn.

'Wow, I'm tired,' she announced.

'Yeah, me too,' Andy said. 'We've had a pretty wild day. Even for a couple of clones.'

'Mmm,' she murmured. She lay down. 'Good-night.'

''Night,' he replied. He stretched out on the ground and closed his eyes.

She waited until his breathing became slow and steady.

Then she sat up. 'Andy?' she said softly. No response. As quietly as possible, she got up – and heard the crackle of a branch she had stepped on. She held her breath.

Andy didn't stir. So much for his superhearing, she thought.

She hurried down the path in the direction of the road. Surely someone would take pity on a ragged, dirty girl standing by the side of a highway in the middle of the night. As for her own safety with a stranger – she'd just have to trust her instincts.

When she reached the highway, she couldn't hear any oncoming cars. But she did see something that lifted her spirits. In the parking area in front of the convenience store, next to the Winnebago, was a black sedan. Mr Devon was waiting for her.

She ran across the highway. As she got closer, she could make out the figure of a man in the driver's seat. And yes, it was Mr Devon!

She rapped on the window. He didn't respond. And when she opened the door, he didn't move.

He couldn't move. Because he was dead.

13

Amy sat huddled on the front step of the store. Flashing lights from two police cars illuminated the darkness of the parking area.

Everything had happened so fast. After finding Mr Devon, she had flagged down a truck. The driver had used his cellular phone to call the police.

'It looks like he was struck with some sort of kick to the solar plexus,' she had heard one of the officers say. 'Whoever did this knew martial arts.'

Then there were the candy bars lying on the ground by the car – candy bars that had obviously fallen out of a big sack of junk food. So when the police officer had asked her if she knew anything, Amy had told him about the boy in the woods.

And now she saw Andy, with a police officer on

either side of him, emerging from the trees. 'Is this the boy?' one of the officers asked her.

'Yes,' she replied, and quickly looked away.

'Amy! What's going on? Tell them I didn't do anything!'

She studied her hiking boots, picked off chunks of dried mud, and tried unsuccessfully to shut out the policeman's voice.

'. . . under suspicion of murder. You have the right to remain silent. Anything you say can and will be held against you in a court of law.'

She heard the clink of the handcuffs, the slam of the car door. Something forced her to raise her eyes and look directly into the back window of the patrol car. She could see Andy, looking in her direction. In the darkness, she could still make out the expression on his face. It wasn't hate, or anger − it was sadness.

She knew he couldn't see her face. He didn't have that kind of power. She said nothing, but that didn't matter either, because he wouldn't be able to hear her anyway.

Unless he could hear the sound of a heart breaking.

As the police car drove out of sight, Amy picked up a conversation between the remaining two officers.

'What about the girl?'

'See if she's got any identification on her, and contact her parents. If she's not from around here, call Family Services and have them take her to a shelter.'

Fortunately, at that moment, the ambulance arrived and the officers became distracted. It wasn't difficult for Amy to slip around the side of the store without alerting them.

As she ran back into the woods, she relied totally on her acute night vision. Not only was she surrounded by pitch darkness, she was practically blinded by tears. She ran and ran until she dropped from sheer exhaustion.

A light rain started to fall. Taking shelter under the thick branches of a leafy tree, she curled up against the truck. She was wet and cold and her legs ached, but she didn't care. Her emotional pain was a lot more unbearable.

Andy . . . the exhilaration of finding him, followed so soon by the agony of his betrayal.

She touched her face. It was wet – not from the rain, but from the tears streaming down her cheeks. She cried for Mr Devon, for Andy. For herself. And finally she cried herself into a dreamless sleep.

Birds woke her before dawn. A faint pink streak

in the grey sky told her the sun would be rising soon, but she couldn't wait for that. She took a moment to examine her surroundings and located the trail they'd taken on their first day.

When she knew she was nearing the campsite, she slowed down. She had no idea what she would find there, but as she emerged from the bushes, she saw the tents. The clearing was silent, and no one was in sight. It was still early enough for them to be sleeping.

Cautiously she made her way to the tent that Dallas and Eric shared and gently pulled back the flap of canvas that served as the door. Eric was inside, alone. He was sleeping, but somehow he must have been aware of her presence. He opened his eyes.

'You're back,' he murmured.

'Yes.'

He started to move, and then he groaned. '*Ow.*'

'What's the matter?'

'I hurt my ankle last night. I think it's sprained.'

She went into the tent and sat down beside him.

A grimace of pain crossed his face as he managed to pull himself into a sitting position. She couldn't be sure if the pain was a response to his ankle or to seeing her.

'Where's your boyfriend?' he asked.

'Who?'

'Andy.'

'He's not my boyfriend, Eric, he never was. And he's not here.'

'Oh.' But his eyes didn't warm up at all.

'How did you hurt your ankle?' she asked him.

Eric almost smiled, but quickly his face went blank again. 'It was pretty stupid. I abseiled all the way down that mountain, twice, with no problems. Then, on the way back to camp, I tripped over a tree trunk.'

'Eric?' Brooke's voice came from outside the tent. 'Is Tasha in there?'

'No,' Eric called out.

Brooke came into the tent. When she saw Amy, her face darkened. 'It's *you*.'

Amy couldn't think of a response. 'Where's Tasha?' she asked instead.

'I don't know,' Eric said. 'She probably went off with Dallas this morning. He wanted to try out one of the mountain bikes.'

'That figures,' Brooke said grumpily. 'She's been teacher's pet since this trip began.'

Eric examined his foot woefully. 'I wonder if I'm going to be able to pedal with this ankle. It's really swelling.'

'Maybe we can go hang-gliding today instead,' Brooke said. 'That would be easier on your ankle.'

Amy's eyes darted back and forth between Brooke and Eric. She and Andy had been gone all night. Hadn't their disappearance bothered anyone?

She couldn't resist asking. 'What did Dallas say when he found out Andy and I were gone?'

Brooke gazed at her haughtily. 'Well, he certainly wasn't happy about it. It doesn't look good for a counsellor if two campers run away. He ditched us to go looking for you, but he gave up pretty quickly. Personally, I don't think he really cared what happened to you.'

Amy couldn't believe it. She and Andy were under eighteen and had been gone since the previous day. Surely that wasn't a normal situation for any Wilderness Adventure programme!

Brooke studied her fingernails in an obvious attempt to look casual and bored as she asked, 'Where's Andy?'

'I don't know.' Amy wanted to tell Eric the story, but not with Brooke there.

Brooke smiled with satisfaction. 'Oh, did you two break up?'

'We were never together,' Amy replied.

'Oh, *please*,' Brooke said. 'We *saw* you, remember?'

'That was a mistake, Brooke. A big mistake. Want to know *how* big? I'll tell you where Andy is right now. He's in jail. Where he should be.'

This got a reaction from Eric. He gasped, and real anger was clearly visible on his face. 'Are you all right? Did he hurt you?'

'No, it's not what you're thinking,' Amy said quickly. 'But – he's not who I thought he was. Please, guys, I really don't want to talk about it. I just need to find Tasha.' She knew Tasha would understand. Do you know where she and Dallas went?'

'Probably back to the mountain we abseiled yesterday,' Eric told her. 'That's where we're all supposed to mountain bike today.'

'Okay.' Amy started out of the tent.

'Amy?'

She turned back to Brooke.

'What?'

'Sorry about the trap.'

'The trap?'

'The animal trap I set in our tent. I didn't really want to hurt you. I just meant to, you know, scare you.'

Amy sighed. Well, at least this was something she wouldn't have to hold Andy responsible for. 'It's okay.'

As she walked away, she heard Eric yelling at Brooke for that stupid stunt. At least he still cared.

Amy hurried towards the mountain they had abseiled. She spotted a set of bike tracks along the way. Maybe Tasha had ridden on Dallas's bike. Amy would have to think of a way to explain her and Andy's disappearance to Dallas, and to find a way to get Tasha alone for the real explanation.

She started to run up the mountain. Soon Dallas came into sight. He was at the top of the drop and his lips were moving. He had to be talking to Tasha, even though Amy couldn't see her.

It wasn't until she was about thirty feet from him that she realised no one was with him. He was talking on a cell phone.

'No, the weather's going to be okay,' he was saying. 'There's still a little fog left, but that should be lifting in the next few minutes. Visibility will be good then. When can you get the helicopter?'

Nothing was making any sense. If Dallas had a cell phone, why hadn't he used it before, when Flora died? Why hadn't he called for help from right here in the woods, instead of carrying Flora down to the convenience store?

The convenience store that wasn't open. In her

distress over Mr Devon and Andy, she'd almost forgotten that fact. How had Dallas alerted an ambulance and the Wilderness Adventure head-quarters? On his cell phone?

Dallas's next words brought her back down to earth with a thud.

'Look, they have to be in the woods somewhere. They couldn't get that far in the dark. Just fly over the area and you'll spot them. We're getting paid big bucks to bring them in, so – Hello? Hello? I can't hear you, the line's breaking up. I'll call you later.'

Dallas tossed the phone into the pack on his back. And saw Amy. 'Hey!'

Her blood went cold, but she didn't run. 'Where's Tasha?'

'Around.' He was eyeing her keenly as if trying to figure out how much of his phone conversation she'd heard. 'Where's Andy? I was getting worried about you two. You were out all night.' He leered at her. 'I won't ask what you guys were doing. I'm just glad you're back.'

Amy moved up the mountain until she was by his side. 'Who hired you?' she demanded.

'What?'

'Who's paying you these big bucks to bring me and Andy in?'

His eyes twitched. 'I don't know what you're talking about.'

'Why did you cut the rope bridge?' she asked. 'That was stupid. Weren't you told that they want us alive? I'll bet you wouldn't have got as much money if we'd drowned.'

'That wasn't my idea, that was—' He stopped.

'Whose?' Amy asked. 'The partner you were just talking to on the phone?'

'None of your business.' He was clearly uncomfortable, though he didn't look scared. 'Come on, we're going back to the campsite,' he said, pulling her by the arm.

Amy wrenched herself away. Startled by her show of strength, Dallas didn't react immediately. Then he stepped closer. 'No more games, little girl. You're coming with me.'

She slammed her foot down on his, knowing she might break a few of his toes. She was right. He howled, grabbed his foot, and started hopping around wildly. She stepped back to get out of his way and fell.

Into the void.

Her scream pierced the air, but the experiences of

the past day hadn't dulled her reactions. She grabbed on to the first ledge that extended from the side of the mountain. And there she hung. The drop was steep – a certain death. And this time there were no ropes around.

Dallas leaned over the side. He was clearly in pain, but he bared his teeth in something that vaguely resembled a grin. 'You're lucky, Amy. Because you were right. I get more money if I bring you in alive.' He had one of the abseiling ropes in his hand and threw it down.

She grabbed it, and pulled hard to give herself the leverage to get her foot onto the ledge. When she was back on the cliff, Dallas grabbed both her hands, much harder this time since he was prepared for her strength, and tied them together with the rope. She struggled, but it was too late. She couldn't use her hands.

Her brain went into immediate rewind. She conjured up the image of Andy defending them from the bear. And before Dallas knew what had hit him, Amy swung out a leg and kicked him square in the face.

Dazed, Dallas lunged at her, but she jumped out of his way. This time *he* went flying off the mountain. Only he didn't have Amy's quick reflexes.

He missed the ledge.

14

Her hands still tied, Amy hurried down the easy side of the mountain. Then she ran around it to the spot where Dallas had landed.

One glance told her there was nothing she could do for him. This guy would never have another opportunity to terrorise Wilderness Adventure participants.

The pack he'd been wearing had broken off from his back, and the contents were spilled all over the place. She could identify pieces of the cell phone, which wouldn't be any help to her now. She also spotted a folder lying a few feet away and was about to retrieve it when a gust of wind sent the papers flying in all directions. As for the gun Andy had claimed Dallas carried, Amy didn't see it.

And she didn't want to hang around and meet Dallas's partner. So she took off.

Without the use of her arms, she couldn't run as fast as usual, but it still didn't take long for her to reach the campsite. Brooke was still in Eric's tent. Amy could hear her complaining even before she got there.

'You know, my parents didn't pay good money for me to sit around doing nothing,' she was whining as Amy tore into the tent.

Amy planted herself next to Eric. 'Untie me,' she demanded.

'What happened?' Eric asked as he released her from the binding rope. 'Where's Tasha?'

'She hasn't come back here?'

'No. Wasn't she with Dallas?' Eric was visibly alarmed. He tried to stand up, wincing as he put some weight on the foot with the sprained ankle. 'We have to go and find her.'

'I think we should wait for Dallas,' Brooke said.

'It'll be a long wait,' Amy said grimly. 'He's lying at the bottom of the mountain. And he won't be getting up anytime soon.'

'Amy!' Eric yelped. 'Did you—'

'No, I didn't push him, he fell,' Amy said impatiently. 'Come on, we have to find Tasha and get out of these woods.'

Brooke didn't move. 'Poor Dallas!' she moaned. 'He was so cute!'

'Yeah,' Amy said. 'He was a very cute bad guy. He was planning to kidnap me and Andy.' She glanced meaningfully at Eric, and she could tell he understood why. Brooke didn't, of course.

'Why would he kidnap you and Andy?'

'Uh, I meant, he wanted to kidnap all of us. He's even arranged for someone to come in a helicopter to find us. So hurry up!'

Eric was on his feet now, but he was clearly hurting.

'Can you walk?' Amy asked him anxiously.

'I can limp,' he said.

They started along the trail that led back to the road. Eric's limp meant that they couldn't move very fast. And now Brooke was frightened. She kept searching the skies for any sign of the helicopter. 'We're never going to get out of here!' she wailed.

Eric was pale. 'You guys go on without me.'

'Okay,' Brooke said, but Amy refused.

'I'm not leaving you.'

175

'Amy, I can't walk.' Eric winced. 'And you're the one the kidnapper really wants.'

'Shhh!' Amy glanced in Brooke's direction. But Brooke was too freaked out to wonder why a kidnapper would prefer Amy to her.

Amy crouched down. 'Eric, get on my back.'

'What?'

'I'll carry you piggyback.'

'Amy!' Brooke screeched. 'He's twice your size!'

'I have an unusually strong back,' Amy said, hoping that would be explanation enough. She was more concerned about whether Eric would agree to travel this way. Would his male ego think it too undignified and unmanly?

Brooke watched openmouthed as Eric hoisted himself onto Amy's back, hooking his legs around her waist and resting his hands on her shoulders.

They could move now. As they walked, they all called out for Tasha, and Amy discovered a talent she hadn't even known she had. Her voice was louder than Eric's and Brooke's combined. She knew she was demonstrating too many unique qualities in front of a girl who didn't – and *mustn't* – know who and what she was. But for once she didn't care. Tasha and Eric would always be more important to her than any secret.

And searching for Tasha kept her from thinking about someone she had treated unfairly. Andy. Andy, who didn't belong in jail. Who hadn't betrayed her. Who, according to Dallas's mission, was exactly who and what he claimed to be. A clone. Like her.

With all these thoughts cluttering her head, it took a moment before a dim, distant noise registered in her mind. It was a whirring, buzzing sound, a low, rough humming.

'I hear a helicopter,' she announced.

'Hide!' Brooke cried. 'We have to hide!'

But there was no time for that. They could all see and hear the helicopter now, and whoever was flying it would be able to see them. There was nowhere to run, nowhere to hide.

Brooke was still wailing. 'Shut up!' Amy ordered her. 'I'm trying to think!' If there was only one man in the helicopter, maybe she could take him on. But he probably had weapons . . .

Eric whispered in her ear. 'I'm sorry. I'm sorry I've been such a jerk.'

Despite the situation, Amy smiled. 'I forgive you.' Then she said, 'I'm sorry I kissed Andy.'

Eric echoed her words. 'I forgive you.'

The helicopter was right over them now, and it was dropping down. The noise of the propellers filled the air. Even so, Amy heard Eric whisper something else.

'I love you.'

It was her turn to echo *his* words, and she could only hope that there would be an opportunity to tell him again when he could hear her.

And then she heard something else. A voice, indistinct, faint, but wonderfully familiar. The voice of someone else who knew she could hear a voice over the sound of a helicopter.

She listened to the instructions. 'We have to return to the clearing,' she shouted.

'What?' Brooke shrieked. 'Are you crazy?'

But she followed Amy, who still carried Eric on her back.

At the campsite, the helicopter that Tasha was in landed to rescue them.

15

Clutching his crutch, Eric hobbled through the door his mother was holding open for him. 'Sit there,' Mrs Morgan ordered him, pointing to the fat armchair with its matching ottoman. 'Put your foot up. Are you hungry? Do you want something to eat?'

'No thanks, Mom.'

'Something to drink?' she continued. 'Magazines? Do you want me to turn on the TV?'

Eric thought it was almost worth the constant throbbing in his ankle to get all this attention and service. He enjoyed the pampering. 'I'm okay, Mom,' he said kindly.

'Well, I'll be in the kitchen if you need me,' she said. 'Making your favourite meat loaf for dinner.'

'Thanks, Mom.' He wondered how long he

could milk his injury, and to what extent. Was there the potential for a PlayStation in this situation?

Tasha came downstairs. 'What did the doctor say?'

'It's just a sprain,' he said, then quickly added, 'A very bad sprain.' He'd take his sympathy anywhere he could get it.

Tasha plopped down on the sofa. 'Did you tell Mom anything?'

'Are you kidding?' he responded.

They shared the kind of smile people with a secret shared.

Their parents, along with Amy's mother, had come up to the small town near the Wilderness Adventure campsite to get them. All they had been told was that unfortunate accidents had killed both their counsellors and the programme had been suspended.

The Morgans had been upset, but so relieved that their kids were safe that they didn't fuss too much or bug them with a lot of questions. Tasha and Eric were able to keep details to themselves. Of course, when the bill for the helicopter rental arrived, they would have to come up with some kind of story to explain *that*.

They'd arrived home last night. At least, the Morgans had come home. Amy and her mother had stayed up north.

Eric glanced out the big picture window, the one with a view of Amy's front door. Tasha answered his unspoken question.

'They're not back yet.'

Eric frowned. 'It's almost six. What's keeping them?'

'You know what's keeping them,' Tasha said. 'Getting Andy out of jail. Now that we know Dallas was the real villain, Amy thinks Andy was for real. Look, Eric, you can't blame her for caring about him. That doesn't mean she's in love with him. He's probably more like a brother to her.'

Eric made a face. 'You didn't see them kiss. Believe me, I'd never kiss *you* like that.'

'She saved your life, Eric,' Tasha pointed out.

'Yeah, I know.' He sighed. 'Actually, *you're* the one who saved everyone.'

Tasha preened. 'You're welcome.'

He looked at his sister with unusual interest. 'How did you know we were in trouble? You were Dallas's biggest fan. Why did you run off?'

'Oh, it was just a feeling I had,' Tasha said airily. 'I have very good instincts, you know.'

Eric rolled his eyes. 'If you've got such great instincts, why didn't you figure Dallas out when we first got there? You were practically kissing his feet!'

'That was just an act,' Tasha assured him. 'I was trying to get close to him so I could figure out what he was really all about.'

'I still don't understand,' Eric began, but then something caught his eye. Amy and her mother were getting out of a taxi. Tasha went to the window and waved. A second later Amy appeared at their door.

'What happened?' Tasha asked her. 'Did you find Andy? Were you able to get him out of jail?'

'He was already gone,' Amy said. She sat down on the arm of Eric's chair. 'He escaped that night. He hasn't shown up in San Francisco, and no one knows where he is.'

'How did he escape?' Eric asked.

Amy smiled slightly. 'They're not sure. It was when they were taking off his handcuffs at the jail. They said he moved faster than any human being they'd ever seen.'

Tasha nodded. 'Then he's really a clone too.'

'I guess. I'm not sure of anything any more. I don't even know Andy's last name.'

'*I* do,' Tasha said. 'It's Denker.'

'How do you know that?' Amy asked.

'Well, um . . .' Tasha looked a little embarrassed.

'Yesterday morning Dallas was going to take me for a ride on the mountain bike. He went back to his tent for something, and left his backpack out. I looked inside.'

Eric was surprised. 'You were snooping in his backpack? How come?'

Tasha gave them both an abashed grin. 'I was just curious. I wanted to find out more about him. Anyway, there was a folder, and I found a letter in it. About Amy and Andy. That's when I knew he was up to something.'

'So it wasn't just your famous instincts,' Eric said.

'No, it wasn't,' Tasha admitted. 'I felt pretty stupid being so wrong about him.'

Amy was sympathetic. 'I was just as stupid about Andy. And it took real courage for you to run off by yourself to get help.'

Eric agreed. 'I didn't know you had guts like that.'

'Neither did I,' Tasha said thoughtfully. 'You know, it's kind of ironic. Remember what the brochure said about challenging yourself, realising your potential, facing your fears, and all that?' She grinned. 'I think I got something from that experience. You guys better not call me wimp anytime soon.'

Amy jumped off the chair arm and went to give her friend a hug. 'Never,' she promised.

Eric watched the two best friends embrace, and he was happy for them. He just hoped his own relationship with Amy would get back to where it used to be.

'Oh, by the way, I brought something back,' Amy said. She dug into her bag and took out what looked like a page from a newspaper. 'I found this in the police station. It's the local newspaper.' She read aloud.

' "The body of a female was discovered buried in a shallow grave behind Highway 61. The deceased has been identified as Flora Mulcahy, a counsellor with Wilderness Adventure. Police are investigating the discovery as a homicide." '

Eric thought about the young woman with the wire-rimmed glasses and the halo of blonde curls. How could such a nice person have been involved with a rotten creep like Dallas? But who knew what attracted any person to another? Never in a million years would he ever have thought he'd fall in love with a clone.

'And listen to this,' Amy continued. ' "A teenage boy was discovered wandering in the woods. He claimed to be half-man, half-savage, who has been living for over a century in the wilderness, where he is considered a superhero. His real identity has not yet been established." '

'Willard!' Eric and Tasha exclaimed.

'At least now we know he survived,' Amy said. She went back to sit on the arm of Eric's chair. 'I guess that ties up all the loose ends.'

'Except for Andy,' Eric said.

'Yes.' Amy nodded. 'Andy Denker.'

There was a wistfulness in her voice that tugged at Eric's heart. 'We can look for him,' he offered. 'We'll get on the Internet. Maybe we can hire a private investigator.'

Amy smiled. 'I think he'll turn up again someday. When he wants to. At least now I know that there *are* Andys out there, somewhere.'

'Yeah,' Eric said. He was trying to sound positive, but Amy must have caught something else in his tone. She reached down, took his hand, and squeezed it.

'But it's even nicer knowing there's only one Eric,' she said.

She squeezed his hand again, and he squeezed back. Even more than his mother's pampering, this was definitely worth spraining an ankle for.

REPLICA

MEMO FROM THE DIRECTOR

TO ALL CONCERNED:
IN REGARD TO THE RECENT ENDEAVOUR, PLEASE BE
ADVISED: D HAS BEEN TERMINATED.